WAVES

Two Short Novels

Masuji Ibuse

Translated by
David Aylward and Anthony Liman

KODANSHA INTERNATIONAL

Publication of these translations was assisted by a grant from The Japan
Foundation.

"Waves: A War Diary" was first published by Kawade Bunkō in 1938 under
the title *Sazanami gunki*. "Isle-on-the-Billows" was first published by Kamakura Bunkō in 1946 under the title *Wabisuké*.

Distributed in the United States by Kodansha America, Inc., 114 Fifth
Avenue, New York, N.Y. 10011, and in the United Kingdom and continental
Europe by Kodansha Europe Ltd., Gillingham House, 38-44 Gillingham
Street, London SW1V 1HU. Published by Kodansha International Ltd.,
17-14 Otowa 1-chome, Bunkyo-ku, Tokyo 112, and Kodansha America,
Inc. Copyright © 1986 by Kodansha International Ltd. All rights reserved.
Printed in Japan.

First edition, 1986   ISBN 4-7700-1745-6
First paperback edition, 1993
93 94 95 10 9 8 7 6 5 4 3 2 1

Contents

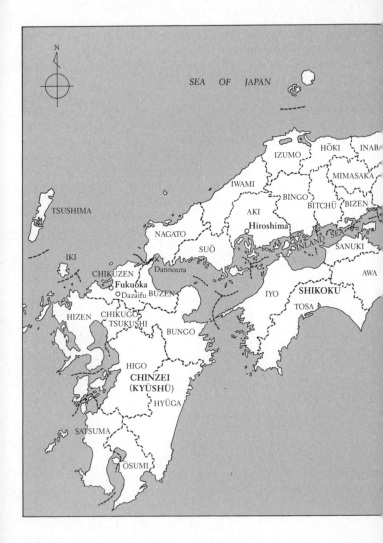

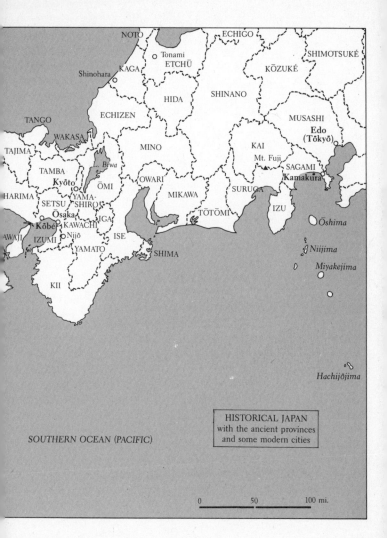

HISTORICAL JAPAN
with the ancient provinces
and some modern cities

SOUTHERN OCEAN (PACIFIC)

0   50   100 mi.

Foreword

There is a growing consensus among Japanese critics that Ibuse Masuji (1898–) is their country's most important living novelist. Like many courageous, experimental artists, Ibuse has had to wait for this recognition. He is now in his late eighties, and although he received prestigious awards—such as the Noma Prize for *Black Rain* and the Cultural Medal—as early as 1966, he has only just come into his own.

Although some of Ibuse's best stories have a rural setting and deal with the hardship of common people's lives, the storytelling itself is characterized by great stylistic sophistication. They may not have a beginning, a middle, or an end in the Western sense, or characters seen in the round, yet every line of a good Ibuse text is polished to a high sheen, pulsing with a powerful rhythm that holds the reader throughout the narrative. Character is revealed by a highly personal, even idiosyncratic, manner of speech rather than by outward description, and this extends well out into the surrounding scenery, which is never merely a background.

Throughout his writing career, Ibuse has consciously and painstakingly developed his craft, sometimes rewriting a finished story years after completion or mercilessly dropping from his collected oeuvre stories that do not meet his very exacting standards. His lifetime's output of fictional works (aside from a body of semidocumentary essays) may be divided into two categories: those that use a "static camera" point of view, and those that use a "moving camera" technique. The first group includes masterpieces like "No Consultation Today" (*Honjitsu kyūshin*, 1950), "Tajinko Village" (*Tajinko mura*, 1939), and "The Station Inn" (*Eki mae ryokan*, 1956), which are well known in Japan—some through film or stage

9

dramatizations—and consequently translated into English. From these, Ibuse emerges as a somewhat nostalgic humanist, who portrays with loving care and deep sympathy a communal way of life that he knew would not last long in the postwar world; he presents a vision of village life with its close human ties, its warmth, and—at times—its cruelty lurking just under the peaceful surface.

Yet Ibuse's sunny face has its colder side: throughout his career he has been interested in dramatic themes of natural or man-made disasters—floods and earthquakes, shipwrecks, brutal civil warfare, and the exile of innocent people to remote penal colonies. His compelling account of the atomic bombing of Hiroshima in *Black Rain* is not an isolated theme that forced itself on him with special urgency, but almost the acceptance of a fateful responsibility; Ibuse happened to be the only artist alive in Japan who was ready for such an overwhelming theme, having over the years developed the style, narrative technique, and philosophy of life required to deal with it. Not only his previous study of men in distress, but the poised, "classical" voice he had learned in his earlier historical tales served him in good stead here, for he needed all the calm detachment he could muster to control an artistic montage of so many cries of agony.

This long series of more dramatic works is best represented by the historical tales, which have not been available to the Western reader. These tales at least partially close the gap between *Black Rain* on the one hand and the translated "village stories" (including brief "gems" like "Salamander" and "Life at Mr. Tange's") on the other; not only because they comment on the human condition in a mature and perceptive way, but because they do so in a uniquely Japanese fashion. In this, despite their tremendous density of unfamiliar historical and geographical detail, they offer a statement more authentic—because less consciously fashioned for Western consumption—than those of more abundantly translated writers like Mishima Yukio, Abe Kōbō, and perhaps even Kawabata Yasunari.

The two stories translated here span a wide historical range, from the late twelfth century to the beginning of the eighteenth. Their protagonists present to the Western reader two major Japanese types: a highborn samurai of the twelfth-century court, and a middle-aged artisan, representing the common people. Despite Ibuse's considerable stylization the interested reader will find here a truer portrayal of the samurai and common people of Japan than the stereotypes usually offered him. Ibuse has adhered to three basic settings throughout his writing career: his native Inland Sea, the scene of "Waves"; the mountains of Kōshū and the Fuji River valley where "Isle-on-the-Billows" takes place; and his adopted home of Tōkyō (old Edo), where other stories are located. These are not a matter of random choice to a writer as meticulous as Ibuse; his best historical tales have a strong sense of authenticity not only because they are so well researched, but because the author is thoroughly familiar with the topography and the atmosphere of his setting. Finally, these two stories offer the widest possible range of narrative technique, or more precisely narrative voice, for which Ibuse is so famous. Although only a limited degree of such stylistic variety will come through in English, it is hoped that the reader will be able to appreciate the somewhat stilted rhetoric of the princeling's diary, which occasionally gives way to the emotional expression of a frightened and confused youngster, in "Waves," and the sober (if ironic) third-person narration of "Isle-on-the-Billows."

The translation aims at a readable, aesthetic accuracy rather than a direct word-by-word rendering of a textual complex that is geographically, historically, and culturally remote. Japanese historical narratives bristle with proper names difficult for a Western reader to remember, especially inherited given names like Tomomori, Yorimori, Moromori, etc., which all sound very similar. Furthermore, there is a custom of referring to the same person by his official title at one point and by his court rank at another. Such designations, for example, as "minister of the Palace Repairs Division" were mostly nominal sinecures given to courtiers and did not mean that the incumbent would actually carry out such duties. Many of these titles not only sound awkward in English, but are actively misleading, since what the nominee may be doing at a given moment quite frequently conflicts with the function of his official post. When we discussed this problem with Mr. Ibuse, he suggested that we change or simplify them according to the logical context and stylistic requirements of the English text. Other changes made were approved by the author. We have tried to put every place name on the appropriate map; some names refer to districts within cities, and consequently will not appear, except in the Notes.

The translators wish to thank the Social Sciences and Humanities Research Council of Canada for several generous grants which made the research for this book possible. Also, our sincere thanks go to friends in Japan who helped to unravel the nuances of Ibuse's style—above all, Prof. Iwasaki Fumito and Prof. Isogai Hideo of Hiroshima, and Mr. Kawasaki Masaru of Tokyo; to Ms. Aoki Yukiko of Tokyo University and Mrs. Naomi Hazell of Toronto, who carefully checked our translation and helped to research the background; and to Mr. John Dunham and Mrs. Joan Morishita for typing the manuscript. Last but not least, we owe a special debt of gratitude to Mr. Ibuse himself, who patiently explained many details of his work and suggested how to solve some of the problems of translation.

Anthony Liman

Waves:
A War Diary

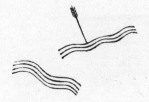

Introduction

At the end of the twelfth century, Japan was on the verge of a new epoch in her history. The samurai did not yet exist as a powerful class, but the coming century would see a new, feudal order of society in which the warrior, not the courtier, was paramount.

The man who forged this new order was Minamoto no Yoritomo, chief of the clan Genji. From Kamakura, his base (a little south of where Edo would stand four hundred years later), he sent his half-brother Yoshitsuné to secure him the capital of Kyōto. Yoshitsuné was a captain of genius, but he had three powerful forces to contend with: the army of his cousin Kiso Yoshinaka, who had preceded him to Kyōto; the other great warrior clan of the Heiké; and the armed monks of the Buddhist monasteries.

Kiso has driven the Heiké out of the capital when the story "Waves" begins, but his talent being more for plunder than for government, he quickly loses popular support, and is defeated and harried to his death by Yoshitsuné. The Heiké, whose point of view the story takes, gained their power thirty years before by routing the Genji in the Hōgen war. Now, however, they have grown soft by emulating the courtly ways of the capital and are no match for Yoshitsuné's spartan troops. They fire the capital and retreat south with the child-emperor Antoku. Eventually, they are betrayed by the so-called cloistered or ex-emperor Goshirakawa (actually a regent), who sides with the Genji to prolong his own shaky power.

The monasteries go along with this arrangement—except for rare individuals like Kakutan in the story—and are content to remain on the sidelines. It is not until four centuries of civil war later that the power of the monks will finally be broken.

15

The Heiké make their last stand at a place called Ichinotani, but are outmaneuvered by Yoshitsuné and scattered across the Inland Sea to the southern islands of Kyūshū and Shikoku. At the final battle at Dannoura (shown in the magically beautiful film *Kwaidan*) the Heiké are exterminated as a clan. In the words of the epic *Tale of the Heiké*: "Yea, the proud ones are but for a moment, like an evening dream in springtime. The mighty are destroyed at last, they are but as dust before the wind. . . ."

But nothing is ever lost in Japan. To this day, along the shores of the Inland Sea, there are whole villages of people believed to be descended from the Heiké, but centuries of reticence for survival's sake have made them reluctant to admit it. As Ibuse himself mentions when he recalls his first impulse to write "Waves":

My friend's sister had a schoolmate from a place in Kyūshū called Gokanoshō. The girl's grandmother apparently used to tell the children: "We have a great secret in our family, but you have to know about it." Then she would take out an old diary and read aloud a few passages from it. . . . Gokanoshō is one of the villages where a group of the Heiké fugitives went into hiding. The grandmother took great pride in their family's lineage, but stressed that it exposed them to social humiliation and must be kept as secret as possible. Yet her granddaughter cared little about that and blurted out the whole story to her schoolmate the very next day.

This diary would have made a valuable historical document about the Genji–Heiké era, but the grandmother apparently never let it past the house's gate. I could only imagine its contents from my friend's secondhand report.

Its author seems to have been a fairly high-placed member of the Heiké clan who was in charge of the family's accounts. He started taking his notes around the time they left the capital, and recorded briefly the main daily events, while reporting in meticulous detail on the flow of the clan's capital. According to his record, as the Heiké enter the West Country, one can gather from the fast diminishing volume of purchases that they are gradually falling into dire poverty.[1]

Yet it is the Heiké about whom the heroic stories are told and written, not their victorious rivals. The exception, curiously enough, is Yoshi-tsuné himself, who was hunted down by his jealous brother and forced to commit suicide. He is portrayed in numerous plays as a kind of Robin Hood, followed into hiding by a small but fiercely loyal band of men. The Japanese, like the English, have an affection for the underdog.

This is the historical background. The existence of the young hero, Taira no Tomoakira (of the Heiké), is historical fact, but otherwise little is known of him except that he gave his own life saving his father in the rout of Ichinotani. Ibuse shows him as a gently reared teenager forced by the fires of war to change from the ways of the court to those of a cynical sea pirate.

This novella has a very special place in Ibuse's writing. It stands out not only as the first and quite likely the best among his stories on historical themes, it is a piece of writing that took him about ten years to complete—much longer than serious novels three or four times its length. Although the first three installments of "Waves" came out between March and July of 1930, Ibuse seems to have started working on it around 1928 and needed eventually nine installments—the longest interval between them being three years—to finish this ambitious work by 1938.

To reach for this particular historical material—so familiar to the Japanese from the classical "martial chronicles" (*gunki monogatari*) such as the *Hōgen*, *Heiji*, and *Heiké monogatari* and their popular stage derivations—and refashion it into modern literature presents a tremendous challenge. A long tradition of dramatizing the principal actors and even the minor episodes of the Genji–Heiké conflict has not only created a detailed awareness of the era, but has conditioned the Japanese reader and theatergoer (for a good deal of the puppet and Nō repertoire derives from the Heiké story) to a fairly orthodox response to their poetic conventions. The high moments of these texts are as well known to the Japanese audience as the popular climactic lines from Hamlet or Lear are to the English; to ignore the rhythm and flavor of these archaic phrases altogether would make little sense even to the most modern-minded reader. On the other hand, a contemporary writer who uses this material is obviously interested in more than just expressing his admiration for this particular narrative rhythm. Using the familiar theme and some of the well-worn ancient imagery he must express his own con-

17

cerns, resetting the archaic verbal icons in a stylistic context that is entirely his own.

Let us see how Ibuse accomplished this difficult task. Like other skillful writers of historical fiction, he chose to keep the better-known historical personalities in the wings of his story's stage. He knew that to let someone like Yoshitsuné become the central character would mean sacrificing either his creative freedom or his deep respect for historical reality as handed down to him by literary tradition. Instead, he lets the historically marginal figure of his young narrator observe the main events and their protagonists from the sidelines, as it were, allowing them to provide the time frame and the dramatic punctuation of the narrative. So the basic outline and setting of the story are given: it happens between the flight from the capital in the Seventh Month (lunar calendar) of 1183 and the debacle of Ichinotani in the Second Month of the following year, and follows the natural escape route to the West Country (i.e. Shikoku and Kyūshū) along the coast of the Inland Sea and the many islands that dot it. Yet within the given limits of time and place, the author has a fairly free hand. The way the plot develops has been likened to a scroll (*emakimono*) technique: one colorful episode follows another, often without the rigid causal relation required by Western aesthetics. Young Tomoakira, although he shares the tastes and preoccupations of his class, is by no means the stereotyped Heian courtier, but rather an alter ago who expresses his creator's feelings and opinions, making the story attractive to the modern reader.

The reason it took Ibuse so long to complete this story is that he had a theme and a stylistic opportunity of such extraordinary potential: he had to develop both as an artist and as a human being to handle it adequately. From the very beginning, he intended to dramatize a young boy's initiation into a cruel world at war (let's bear in mind that he started writing this novella on the eve of the Manchurian Incident and finished it on the eve of World War II), and to show how quickly one has to "grow up" in such an abnormal situation. And young Tomoakira does age fast, almost too fast considering the story spans only ten months or so. From a pampered aristocratic youth whose roughest pastime used to be a game of *kemari* (a ritualized slow-motion version of soccer), he is forced to become a leader of desperate marauders, running away from the familiar

18

cultivated world of the capital to a wilderness of rough fishing villages and camps in the forest.

While at the outset of his ordeal the boy is terrified by the Genji ruffian who comes to challenge his father, toward the end of the story he calmly admires the "elegant display of skill" with which the monk Kakutan "sent five heads flying." Not that Ibuse is suggesting this "manly toughness" is admirable—note how differently the boy reacts during his two encounters with young girls: the one at Tomonotsu who offers him those juicy pears in her garden and the girl Chinu at Kusuné's estate. With the first, he is still fresh emotionally and perhaps still too sensitive for his own good. At the time of his flirtation with the other, he can hardly remember that a town called Tomonotsu existed—it's just another harbor town, one of the many that the exigencies of war make them raze to the ground. Yet while young Tomoakira loses some of his fine courtly sensibility, he certainly does not become blind to the great social upheaval he sees around him. From the very beginning he is somewhat aloof—perhaps to write his diary he needs a considerable distance from the older leaders of his clan—or, if you wish, able to see the weakness of his own class more critically (almost too critically for a teenager). This is where Ibuse's imagination enjoys freest play and where it most departs from classical models such as *The Tale of the Heiké*. Nowhere in the Heiké epic would we find a sarcastic parody of a senior Heiké general's cowardice, as in the scene where the hero's father Tomomori sends out a dull-witted proxy to fight for him and even tries to teach him an " 'extemporaneous' tanka."

The senseless brutality of war is always somewhat stylized and beautified in the classical *gunki monogatari*. Ibuse not only satirizes their stereotyped, sentimental conventions, but presents a realistic view of combat that must have been much more savage than the pretty ritual portrayed in the *emakimono* and the *gunki monogatari*. Setting the perceptions of the common people, or perhaps simply their common sense—the boy often tries to identify with this view—against the narrow mentality of the ruling establishment shapes Ibuse's imagery in a certain way: rather than the elegant, dance-like ritual of warfare we see in the *haute culture* of the epic tales or the scrolls, Ibuse shows us a brutal parody with the raw punch of a rural puppet show, as in the bareback rider episode. At other times, as Yasuoka Shōtarō suggests,[2] his fighting men seem to come from a much older world, resembling the divine warriors of myth, such as Susanoo no Mikoto.

Yet even the starkest of these images are conveyed by a highly polished style. Ibuse did not spend the long waiting years between the writing of "Waves" in vain: what really makes the young diarist's rapid emotional change credible is the changing, "maturing" style of the narration itself. In the beginning, the boy's writing is fairly subjective, at times even sentimental. He still sees the world through the hazy veil of his youthful memories, which make the present but a shadow of things past. Many a time he sees things as they might have been, had the world not changed so drastically. Yet change it did, and the tone of the boy's reflections around the middle of the narrative starts changing too, though in the subtlest of ways. One notices that by the end there are few frills in his laconic entries and no "poetry," only a tremendous fatigue and a clearheaded, pragmatic estimate of the resources left to him.

Reading Ibuse's sophisticated and thoughtful style—even its somewhat faded reflection in English—we must watch for the nuances, for he is not a writer who rushes ahead on the crest of a wave of words along the line of a clear plot. Quite the contrary; he will dwell on the shape and depth of every sentence until he feels it is perfect, even at the risk of sluggish pace at times. But where does the excitement and the strong sense of rhythm come from, then? The writing is spare and there are lacunae between the sentences where a lot remains unsaid. Some lines, especially when Ibuse draws a stylized caricature, are energetic and robust; yet others are very fine, almost invisible, by contrast. It is this interplay and harmony of shaded line that is difficult to perceive, because to the casual reader only the thick line of caricature stands out. What we tend to call "vignettes" are often important sections of the narrative scroll, contributing to its rich variety and consequently to the fullness of our reading experience. Take for example the little episode about the old groom:

> A little apart from this bustle, General Shigehira's old groom crouches by himself. With a stout black helmet on his head and a small blade in one hand, he is solemnly cutting dry grass for his

master's horse. A clump of grass is left where a broken arrow sticks in the ground. Anxious to avoid the missile, he has carefully cut all around it.

While the image of an old man cutting carefully around the broken arrow (instead of simply pulling it out and throwing it away) bears the unmistakably Ibuse touch of caricature, it tells the reader a lot about the old man's mentality: he respects his masters' tools of war so much that he daren't touch them, preferring his own tool and not wanting anything to do with the sinister place where the arrow has struck.

Yet even when Ibuse parodies the lyrical accounts of the Heiké's glory and tones down the pathos of their downfall, the ancient images still carry enough weight and luster to give an essentially modern story the sad elegance of bygone days. Furthermore, the historical disguise—the theme's safe distance from the topical issues of the present—allows the contemporary author to maintain an aesthetic control and perhaps even overcome some of his "bad habits." Ibuse had to contend with two powerful influences at this point in his career: the *watakushi shōsetsu* (I-novel) technique as the prevailing mode of Japanese writing on the one hand and the pressures of leftism in the literary establishment on the other. It would be very easy to dismiss such pressures as irrelevant to a truly independent artist. But we must not forget that Ibuse is Japanese and as such struggles for his independence in ways different from ours. He had tried his hand at Western techniques of storytelling before "Waves" and even managed to work out a reasonable compromise between traditional Japanese ways of handling the first-person narrative and those used in the West. Yet he is too serious an artist to imitate foreign modes, when there are viable native ones that can be modified to modern expectations. He couldn't dismiss the "confessional mode" altogether, for he felt it provided an authentic, credible voice, a voice that could speak most intimately to a reader living in a confused age where the objective, wide-focus narration of the omniscient writer has lost much of its authority.

Yet unlike the self-pitying I-novelists of the orthodox school, Ibuse manages to preserve a considerable distance between his own self and the projected "I" of his young narrator—there is a skillful insertion of another "I" (the "translator" and editor) between the two—while maintaining the close focus, the fine perception, and the convincing subjective experience of the Japanese first-person narrative. Moreover, by placing his story—so remote in terms of time—in the familiar landscape of his childhood, he can indulge in a sort of lyrical excursion into the favorite scenery of his own past, without being too obviously nostalgic. When we look carefully at the hero's "coming of age" and the painful choices this process involves, we can see how much of the writer's own dilemma is symbolically represented. The boy is forced to become a man faster than he likes and he badly needs a father figure to identify with. As frequently happens in real life, his own father is disqualified by his unattractive qualities, and he has to turn either to the staunch and brave but hopelessly rustic Miyaji Kotarō (almost foolish in his sincerity) or to his opposite, the well-read and ingenious, if somewhat cynical, monk Kakutan. Two models of courage, two "ways of the warrior" to follow—will young Tomoakira choose the good-natured, conservative representative of the good old countryside or will he follow the cooler, more efficient "city intellectual" Kakutan? Precisely the kind of decision Ibuse himself had to make as a young man: should he remain in his native village (Innoshima, Miyaji's native island, is very close to Ibuse's birthplace and one of his favorite islands) and become a provincial gentleman-farmer who dabbles in the arts, or should he give it all up and go to the cold, foreign land of the Tokyo *bohème* and become a modern artist? As a larger metaphor, the hero's choice between these two possible models of identity may be seen as symbolic of the Japanese situation at the outset of World War II, which was definitely a historical crossroads for that country. Just as the young boy—whether he likes it or not—eventually comes to act like Kakutan because his is the more efficient, "modern" way, while gallant old Miyaji dies a heroic death, so Japan emerged from the war with a cooler and more cynical sense of identity than the slightly naïve prewar one.

The lofty historical theme and the diary format not only helped Ibuse bypass the pitfalls of the I-novel, they also enabled him to develop the classical poise and the aesthetic control needed to restrain the emotional turmoil he must have felt when virtually all his literary friends joined the popular proletarian literature movement in the late twenties, and he—ironically enough the only one among these intellectuals who had a genuine interest in the common people—was left in complete isolation. One does feel the loneliness and the longing for communication with human beings outside his own class throughout "Waves," yet these feelings are mostly well integrated into the story and do not become self-serving ideological motifs.

"Waves" is one of those rare, completely successful works of art which emerge once or twice in an artist's lifetime. A tremendous wealth of meaning blends with precise, realistic detail; colorful images of the heroic past are imbued with contemporary significance; and an entire poetic tradition is subjected to loving parody and thus to a critical reinterpretation, welding the best in the elegant tradition of the past to modern, enlightened skepticism.

1. Ibuse, postscript in *Sazanami gunki*, Tokyo, Sakuhinsha, 1980, p. 168.
2. Yasuoka Shōtarō, postscript in Ibuse, op. cit., p. 191.

Editor's note: Explanatory notes, arranged according to page number, can be found at the end of the book. Japanese names (except on the title page and jacket) follow the Japanese order—given name last.

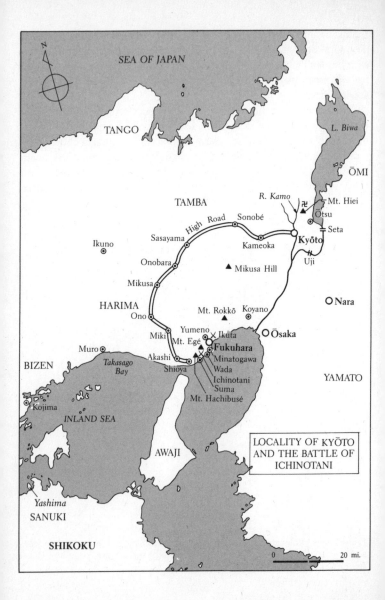

LOCALITY OF KYŌTO
AND THE BATTLE OF
ICHINOTANI

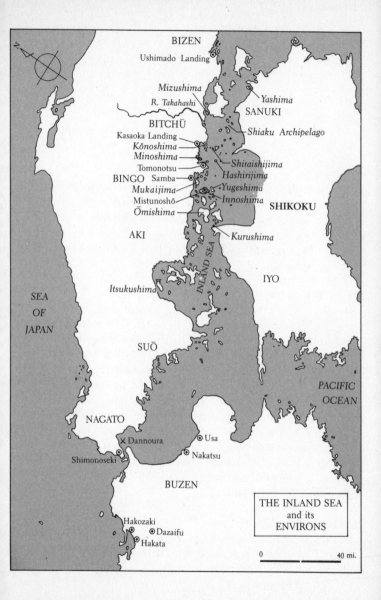

THE INLAND SEA
and its
ENVIRONS

0   40 mi.

Waves: A War Diary

In the Seventh Month, lunar calendar, of the second year of the Juei period (A.D. 1183), the people of the renowned Heiké clan were driven by the fortunes of war to desert the capital—at that time, Kyōto. An account of their flight has been left to us by a certain young man of the same family. I present part of it here translated into a less archaic style.

Second Year of Juei, 15th Day of the Seventh Month:
– Harada, Kikuchi, and Matsura led a body of over three thousand horse into the capital last night. They return from putting down the rebellion in the southern island of Kyūshū. In the courtyard of Lord Yorimori's residence here in the Rokuhara, I caught a glimpse of Harada and Matsura, their figures lit up in the glow of watch fires. Harada looked splendid on his black horse, nearly standing in the stirrups, every inch the triumphant general. Yet we could guess how much foul weather and fierce battle his faded red cape had seen, and felt sorry for him. Kikuchi was on foot, wearing armor laced in light green and a horned helmet, carrying a cane-bound bow and two dozen arrows with eagle's-feather fletchings. A black-whiskered foot soldier was steadying his horse—a sturdy animal of pure white coat, it was. Champing for the charge even there, in that quiet firelit garden!

16th Day of the Seventh Month:
– Bad news. The army we sent to pacify the north was trapped in a valley in Etchū and almost wiped out. There were over eight thousand dead and wounded.

The city in great distress—every door and gateway shut, and masses for the dead held without break the day long, bells tolling and tolling . . . the prayers of one house drowned out by the prayers of the next. Those of the widows are loudest.

Why don't we pull down the bridges at Uji and Seta? We *must* act together! When I asked General Shigehira, he said to me, "It's not just the capital this time; there is danger everywhere. Part of Kiso's army already prepares to invade the city. As for the bridges, Kiso is about to pull them down himself to guard his rear against a larger force on its way from the east. By now it may be too late to do anything but save the young emperor and leave the city to the Genji. . . ." I saw tears in his eyes, and the three little children beside me began to cry.

Outside, we can hear the racket of people and horses and carts hurrying by our walls. Much running back and forth from Lord Yorimori's residence. Our chaplain, panic-stricken by these alarums, came to us babbling some nonsense about wouldn't we like our valuables taken to the manor of a person in Bizen named Seno-o? He was on intimate terms with one of his retainers and would undertake to see that transportation was inexpensive, etc., etc. We only laughed at him. Weren't there twenty thousand of Kiso's cavalry massing near East Sakamoto on Mt. Hiei?

Our poor chaplain was so crestfallen he ran off again, carrying a halberd in his right hand and ringing a bell in his left. Apart from his usual brown habit, he wore only a helmet to protect himself.

– Very hot today. I had thought the leaves on the plantain in our garden the same size as always, but when I looked just now, they were twice as large as last year's, with firm blossoms glowing in their shade.

17th Day of the Seventh Month:

– I heard a loud voice outside the gate, and went to peer over the wall. A large man mounted bareback was shouting something at us. His provincial accent was hard to follow, but the drift seemed to be:

". . . I am Kiso Yoshinaka's man from the province of Shinano! Since I left home, my enemies have never defeated me—not in the battles of Omi and Aida, in sieges of strongholds at Tonami, Kurosaka, Shiosaka, and Shinohara in the north, nor at the gates of the capital, guarded by your monkish rabble. . . ," and so on—a fellow named Naruo, it seemed. "Ever since the Hōgen business, the treachery of you Heiké has disgusted me! The master of your house must be a high-ranking general; if he has any guts, he'll open his gate and come out and fight! Is he afraid?"

He wore nothing but a dark blue jerkin held together with a ragged corselet. His bamboo quiver had only three arrows, and as he waved his bow I noticed the string had been cut and retied. The thick beard sprouting on his cheeks and jaw, and a hood-like thing covering his head, made him look about fifty, but on further scrutiny I thought he could have been as young as twenty. There was mud on the tip of his horse's long tail, and only three of its hooves were shod.

Our people were thrown into confusion by this strange visitor. By now there were others watching him over the wall with me.

In this kind of situation, it was naturally up to my father to accept the challenge, but instead, with a distracted expression, he called a certain Saburōji to him. Promising to give his younger brother four rolls of Hachijō silk if anything happened, he persuaded the poor devil to don his master's armor. Saburōji, being a little slow of wit, asked my father— who was trying to teach him an "extemporaneous" tanka—again and again for instruction while the armor was being put on. By the time he was dressed, Saburōji seemed to have memorized the poem, and mounted his borrowed horse. This was a spirited beast, able to make the foolish retainer look like a proud Heiké commander departing for battle.

For an adequate memorial of Saburōji's heroic figure, I must give some account of his apparel. His mount had a saddle of the *ikakeji* type, with gold dust sprayed over a black lacquer base, and his tea-colored robe had a rock-landscape design worked in yellow thread, and flying plovers in white. Over this he wore a corselet of purple tint, darkening toward the tassets. A horned helmet and a sword with gilt mountings completed his equipage.

The gate was opened and Saburōji cantered out into the square. Turning toward his bareback adversary, he instantly charged. I was sure his big black broad-chested charger would knock the other's down. To my amazement, Saburōji's horse veered sharply aside, made a complete circle around the other, and came to a halt. The challenger must have used the bow like a whip, and beat him off by slashing his mount across the nose.

The two now faced each other, glaring. The bareback rider surprised me again by pulling out a kind of pole he'd been carrying at his side, before bellowing the same challenge we heard previously. He carried no sword, and I thought: our champion can't fail to down him.

Saburōji was silent for a moment after the other had finished. Most likely he'd forgotten the poem my father taught him, but his warlike bearing could not be faulted. He rose in the stirrups, spread his arms wide, and called in a stentorian voice:

"Let those watching from a distance hearken to my words, and those nearby look well. I am famous among the Heiké as Vice-Councillor Tomomori, a warrior equal to a thousand men. Come, and strike quickly if you can!"

He was announcing himself in a very inflated manner, but it was with just such phrases as my father would use on the field of honor. Saburōji twice looked back at us while he was speaking. As soon as he had finished, the two of them engaged. The other was the more powerful by far. He gripped one shoulder with his left hand and Saburōji's helmet with the right, and, wrenching it around, actually tore his head off! A tremendous spurt of blood gushed out of the stump fully four feet into the air, drenching the trunk in red and splattering the ground about. The victor picked up Saburōji's sword and tied it to his horse's reins. The black horse stood steady, as though its will were lost with its master, so keeping the headless body in the saddle.

The bareback rider was after all nothing but a thief. He snatched up Saburōji's casque by one horn and waved it violently around to get rid of the head. When it had fallen out, he stuck the helmet on his own head.

It was too much. I shrank behind the wall and shut my eyes tight. How can such barbarities be allowed to happen? How I hate war! And this is only the beginning. . . .

18th Day of the Seventh Month:
– I forgot to mention yesterday that Saburōji's vanquisher made off with his horse and armor.

Cannot understand Father's attitude. He says Saburōji had to be sacrificed for the sake of our family and the clan as a whole. I *hate* that kind of sophistry and pity his lack of courage.

– It is past midnight now. When I spent the night in a temple at Uzumasa last year, the splashing of the brook and the sighing of leaves and branches in the forest disturbed me, and I couldn't sleep. Now I'm sleepless for the opposite reason: too much quiet.

Couldn't sleep last night either. I heard the clash of arms outside the gate, then abrupt silence. The sound was no more than two or three sword strokes, but I knew that in the moment following someone had died. Perhaps I shall hear the same sound tonight. . . .

– They say Kiso has upwards of fifty thousand horse. My father thinks warrior-monks from the monasteries on Mt. Hiei will attack us first. Recently, ten senior nobles of the clan sent a proclamation to them, but the priests ignored it. It is said they have already agreed to assist Kiso. We had no warning of it, but my father puts it down to our own delays.

Even if we avoid individual destruction, taking the tonsure and escaping in disguise to join the priests would be worse than useless, in my opinion. They are no more than an offshoot of our own class, even if they have allied themselves with the coming race. The monasteries are all that will be left of the old order, while we are digging our own graves. The fortune-tellers on Third Avenue would say that is exactly what they mean by the Mills of the Gods.

19th Day of the Seventh Month:

– Preparations afoot for our departure; conferences all day long at Lord Yorimori's residence. We may have to fire the city; if so, everything we did here has been wasted effort. Father says he'll miss even the smallest leaf of the fragrant orchid growing on the *nagi* tree in our garden. On the tenon of one of the great pillars of the reconstructed Suzaku Gate at the palace, my name is carved in three places, from when I was a child. No doubt that will burn with everything else. I once saw the glowing remains of one of those red-painted pillars—it looked like a giant steel pole blazing white-hot and spewing out flames.

In everything we did, we used to boast our Rokuhara style, down to the last detail, from the way we wore our court hats to the lining of our kimonos. . . . Dear Rokuhara! You were the mother and father of us all.

20th Day of the Seventh Month:
– Another of Kiso's braves at the gate today. More ferocious than the last, they say—I didn't go out to see him. They won't stop till they've taken everything we have! No appetite today: I'm too frightened.

21st Day of the Seventh Month:
– Another challenge. They offer no harm to the women and children; it's against their code. Such men must be valiant in war.

22nd Day of the Seventh Month:
– Three Kiso retainers came this time. The spirit of our clan has turned into an ailing monster whose fingers and toes are falling off, its bowels turned to water. But what can we do?
– Set off this afternoon for the lord chamberlain's house with a letter from my father. Five samurai rode with me. On the way, we encountered one of Kiso's apes, just by the back gate of the Haimatsu estate. His borrowed outfit of court cap à la Rokuhara, wide sleeves, and culottes with weighted hems looked very ill on such a pugnacious fellow; yet he stared from his carriage with a wonderful hauteur. He must have been bribed by some minister to visit his offices. The ox pulling him was a superb animal, and argued a first-class groom such as are found only near the capital. Catching sight of us, he began to fan himself in an affected manner. As we came abreast, he kept a watchful eye on us, ready to retaliate if we made any hostile moves. He was asking his groom, "You there, am I using this thing right? Don't I look like one of them city toffs?" and plied his fan more briskly still.

This comical speech made us all burst out laughing. He roared out "Stop the carriage," jumped from the back of it sword in hand, and came after us with a shout. One of my men dealt with this hothead by hacking his arm off. It lay in the dust by itself, hand still tightly gripping the sword hilt. I restrained my guards from killing the unfortunate fellow, who promptly deserted his severed arm and disappeared around the corner of an adobe wall.

A little shaken by this incident, I hastened on to the lord chamberlain's residence, where I found a group practicing on their flutes.

25th Day of the Seventh Month:
– I hear that late last night Ex-Emperor Goshirakawa, in his customary monk's habit, left the palace accompanied only by his master of stables; no one knows where. . . .

(Passage omitted. —Author)

Everyone in the clan escorts young Emperor Antoku out of the city today, led by the former minister Munemori. Father hums favorite verses to himself on the way, trying to look calm, but I can see he's not in his best form. A sack of gold dust is tied to his saddle, but it has split, and the golden grains dribble steadily away without his noticing.

A long journey lies ahead of us—by now about seven thousand riders— but not one knows our exact destination. The evening sun is setting in front of us. After it has gone down, the red glow in the sky over the capital lights up the backs of drooping men on horses. When one of them looks over his shoulder, the light seems to bring out the sadness in his face. As we were leaving the city, the Rokuhara and Komatsu estates, the clan mansions on Fourth and Eighth Avenue, our retainers' houses, and all fifty thousand of the common people's dwellings in the Shirakawa district were fired at once. Yet none of us is in a hurry to leave.

Kept falling asleep on my horse, and my escort had to look out for me. – Written down in camp the same evening.

27th Day of the Seventh Month:
– Some of our troops deserted last night. Nobody blames them; we ourselves don't know where we're going.

May be the twenty-eighth today; don't know for sure. I didn't want to ask because it would only sadden my companions. Dates are for people who still have hope.

All I know is that we arrived at the old temporary capital of Fukuhara late last evening. Until three summers ago, it was my home, too. In those days, I thought of nothing but running up and down its stone-paved streets. I remember my shoes made a sliding sound that echoed pleasantly from the earthen walls lining both sides. How I loved to kick my ball down those streets and run after it! Only a short time ago, but now moss coats all the flagstones and every type of grass imaginable has sprung up in the cracks. Cranesbill, plantain, *susuki*, and patrinia are flourishing.

Everyone sleeps in a different place. I've been put up at a beachside villa. Like all the buildings here, it's a ramshackle place with crooked eaves and corridors full of seabirds fluttering back and forth. I can see the stars through the holes in the roof—and the moon, too!

28th Day of the Seventh Month:
– Or perhaps it's the twenty-ninth. The old palace was fired early this morning. From there the blaze spread to the Clear Spring Palace, the Pine-shaded Mansion, and the imperial stables, then to the two-storied Hall of Balconies and the snow-viewing pavilion, and finally to the hillside villa and my own shelter. All were burned down. The thick coat of ivy clinging to my fence was just beginning to turn the deep color of autumn when the flames came, curling and cracking it to a mass of dead leaves. . . .

We have to go to common people's houses to buy rice. A roll of silk gets a little over five bushels; cheaper than the market price in Kyōto, they say. At one house, an old woman asked me why the old capital was being burned. I had no answer, and merely urged her to leave the area.

Shipping of all sizes was assembled on the coast. Someone had fortunately taken the initiative. Struggling to keep ahead of each other, people quickly embarked and rowed off to sea. Rumor has it Kiso's advance guard is right behind us.

– We had just gone about half a mile in our own boat when I noticed three horsemen trying belatedly to join us. They rode straight into the water, waving and calling for us to wait.

We soon descried a body of a score or so men galloping down the beach after them: some of Kiso's scouts. A couple of our archers tried a long shot from the boat. The enemy came on at speed and replied, using the three latecomers for a target. Their shafts pierced deep into the water and bobbed end-up to float quietly on the surface. Although it made no difference, the pursuers went on maneuvering around the beach quite as cheerfully as if they'd been practicing horseback archery at their stables!

No one hurt in this little withdrawal. The three stragglers held their bows high and pressed after us. When near enough, they vaulted out of their saddles onto the boat, trailing seawater from wet armor; turned out to be the governors of Owari, Nagato, and Bitchū.

Their mounts were now abandoned to the elements, and the poor beasts stared after their masters with mute appeal. But our craft—not to mention the others—was already so packed with men and horses there was no room for more. We waved our bows and shouted to send them back to the beach, but they wouldn't leave their masters and continued to follow the boat. Necks raised high, they neighed after us shrilly, again and again. As the rays of morning sunlight picked out their reflections, they and their three mirror images made novel patterns on the water. The animals were tiring, and labored painfully in their swimming.

Nagato nocked an arrow and made to shoot his mount, muttering that from what he knew of its character it might well come after him till it drowned. But he couldn't do it. Instead, he leaned his bow against the gunwale, pleading a wet string. We were just as glad he didn't shoot.

Owari's horse was not such a good swimmer. It slowly fell behind and gave up, turning back to the beach. When it reached the shallows, it scrambled to its feet and whinnied after us twice more.

I wasn't there when the last of the three—Bitchū's—was lost sight of. Most likely it weakened and went under. It had a cream-colored coat, I remember. . . .

16th Day of the Eighth Month:
– General Shigehira terribly seasick. He tried to lean over the side and wash himself with seawater, but it was no use: he was so woebegone he didn't have the strength. I'd been sick myself, but was still able to scoop up some water to rinse out my mouth. We leaned over the side together, but he only pretended to rinse his mouth, saying that salt water was poisonous. Since all our ships are short of drinking water, everyone is agreed on making it last. But the general ordered his aide to bring a full measure of water for me, which I drank.
– A galley was dispatched to shore yesterday to draw fresh water, but by evening had not returned. I remember her name—the *Dragon's Head*—from the bold letters inscribed on her hull. We slackened speed and waited, but this morning there was still no sign of her. Narizumi

suggests that her crew have deserted and left our men without any means of getting back. At this, all are silent, neither supporting nor rejecting his idea. They must be thinking that everyone on board has gone ashore and left us to our fate.

17th Day of the Eighth Month:
– We have advanced in line abreast with the young emperor's flagship all day. Something that looks like a model of the palace has been assembled near her bow. Narizumi asked her crew who had built it. They replied that "Kuromaru" had. And who might he be? was the next question. One of the sailors rowing said *he* was Kuromaru. Admitted he'd never seen a palace, and feared his own version mightn't measure up to court standards. Narizumi went on to ask what that thing decorating the roof was. Kuromaru declared it was his idea of a pair of phoenixes fashioned from ship's timber. Now Narizumi himself, being a country samurai from Awaji, knows nothing of what an emperor's residence looks like. The general decided the man was talking too much and called him over to confer some trifling official title on him. Narizumi was so delighted his excitement lasted till nightfall and he went on talking with the Kuromaru fellow quite late! From the conversation, I gathered our rank and titles were held in the highest esteem. Could they attain such exalted positions, they said, they would never think of returning to their villages.

I knew their hopes were ridiculous. Yet I reflected: were they *not* covetous of our rank, how could we hope to rule them? As it was, they fought for us, obeyed our laws, and freely endured much misery on our account.

– Nightfall, and we've dropped anchor near a small island. After lashing our ships together with mooring lines, we came ashore, leaving five men-at-arms on guard. These know nothing of seafaring, and there is no danger anyone will leave the island. We can sleep peacefully.

The island is called Minoshima. We shall rest here tomorrow.

18th Day of the Eighth Month:
– There are three hills on the island, and a bamboo grove in the hollow between them. I walked through it to one of the hills that was nearly flat on top. In a little meadow there, behind some bushes, I discovered

the chief councillor of Uji taking a rest! He is an old man, but one of our best.

He sat there with legs flung out, busily chewing on something. His white beard was stained and dirty, and waggled back and forth with his jaw movements. He asked me if I wasn't weary of sailing every day. I said no, but I complained of constant seasickness. He invited me to sit down and stretch my legs out.

"I'm an old man with little time left," he said. "I don't know why I should be so eager to live on like this, myself. But I suppose no one can answer that question. Nor does anyone know where we can escape to."

He patted my head kindly and asked me how old I was. He then confessed that being seen eating out here in his nightgown was a painful embarrassment to him.

Our island is in the mouth of a large river. The current strikes it and parts to either side, pouring out to sea in two streams.

19th Day of the Eighth Month:
– Nightfall at the port of Tomonotsu, an ancient but prosperous-looking harbor town. We march up in full battle array, our young men as well as the ladies lightly made up. The townsfolk kneel by the road-side to welcome us. Had they shown signs of resistance, of course, we should have put their entire village to the torch.

Having built a small observation tower as quickly as possible on a hill behind the town, we leave a body of troops to occupy it and set up our main camp at the foot of the same hill. From the slope above, they are an imposing sight.
– I notice a pear tree in the garden of one cottage, with a young girl standing beneath it. I urge my horse up the slope and across the garden. Her eyes, black and glistening like persimmon seeds, are startled as she sees me. Her hair is clumsily arranged in the Rokuhara mode. Most like-ly she saw our Heiké ladies this morning, and is trying to imitate their fashions. How can she know it isn't simply a stylish coiffure, but one used only by married women at the imperial court! She hides behind the trunk of the tree, forcing me to rein in my horse to get a better look at her. I catch just a little of her blushing face as it peers round at me,

but it's a very pretty one. A mounted warrior from the capital must be a striking spectacle. Is she falling in love with me, perhaps? I address her in the speech of Rokuhara.

"That fruit looks ready to eat, but the pears of the capital weren't ripe when I left. It must be mid-autumn already!"

She hides her face completely behind the tree before she answers.

"Wasn't it dangerous, riding uphill s'fast? Pears aren't full ripe, but help yourself if you're thirsty." Her country accent is charming.

I dismount, hand her the reins. She is quite shy, but not enough to run back to the house. Pale with fright, she holds the reins by the end, ready to dash away the instant my horse is restive. After making sure her father and brothers are away, I use a bamboo pole to thrash the branches of the tree. Pears bounce off my horse's head and saddle onto the ground, the firm fruit striking with a juicy sound I find refreshing. I beat harder at the tree, and more and more pears rain down, right at the girl's feet. She shuts her eyes in alarm, but when some of the fruit strike her shoulder, she makes no move. . . .

Same day, evening:

– I see her at the time and place I promised. To elude the watch in case they question me, I turn out in the same outfit as theirs. We meet on a beach at the foot of a cliff, which may soon be covered by the tide. The girl must know the exact hour of low water, but still, she might have chosen a more suitable place for a tryst!

To excite her emotions about our liaison, I ask her why she chose a place so much at the mercy of wind and water. "You want to see me for such a brief time?" I say playfully. "Won't the tide reach us any minute?" She stares in surprise, then jerks her head back and forth. A sigh escapes her as she looks down; she is crying quietly.

Hanging above an island across the way, the moon is half full. Of course, I have seen it often in the capital, but never with this red, metallic glow. Its light catches the girl's hair and neck as she holds her head away from me. I notice she has applied makeup to the nape. Whether because she had only the one mirror or put it on too hurriedly, it does not look well. But at least her coiffure, bathed in moonlight, more

37

closely resembles the correct Rokuhara style than it did at noon.

To dry her tears, I praise the skillful dressing of her hair and how well it suits her. My voice shakes a little, I don't know why. Soon she stops crying and admits her mother assisted at her toilette.

On such a beach, she says, no one will hear if we speak a little louder. I tell her I don't mind if sea spray dampens my clothes. She is just as unconcerned about hers. We put our hands on each other's shoulders.

"Can no one see us here?" I ask. I feel a tremor of passion race through her at my question. Raising her eyes to the cliffs above my head, she reaches around very shyly to stroke my back—so modestly, her elbow no more than grazes my sword hilt. My hand is on her arm. Once, in the capital, I saw a couple hold just such a pose in a Bugaku dance.

Motionless, we stand there on the beach: she with her elbow on my sword hilt, looking patiently up at the cliffs, I with my hand on her arm. I shall put her words down in the Rokuhara way, the true accent being difficult to show:

"Is it not foolish, trying to save your life by placing it in greater danger? I have no right to ask favors of you, but perhaps you can grant me a small one: when you are in battle, please take always the least dangerous position. . . . You leave at dawn tomorrow—never, I think, to return. I know you must give all your mind to fighting, and dare not ask you: think of me. But if you decide to forget war and leave your post forever, remember how happy it will make me. I would come to you then wherever you might be. . . . Why is it, I wonder, that I so much love a man I shall never see again?"

Speaking thus boldly, she stares curiously at my sword hilt; then, asking if the spray won't rust it, begs me to let her draw it out a little.

I should be impressed by her pure heart, but the smell of her clothes and hair moves me to rapture. I put my hand on her shoulder again, feel her pleasure in it, hope she will whisper some little pleasantries in my ear. How strange I so desire the favor of a person below my station!

Next day:
– The local people have come out to watch our departure.

Most of them crowd together, but a score of young girls stand apart, all in chosen places. Each tries to catch her lover's eye and remind him of her loneliness. An equal number among the five thousand of us feel the poignant longing of those glances. But when we board ship, no one so much as waves a hand. I want to make her some sign, but I control myself. Finally, on the pretext of retying a cord of my armor, I lift my hand as high as my shoulder. She runs a few steps forward to raise her own hand shoulder-high. When our ship reaches the tip of a cape and changes course, she is lost from sight.

As we sail past a vessel carrying women of the court, I notice an old lady scolding a young one. The younger woman hangs her head, weeping softly and demurely.

– A little after noon our craft sails into a sheltered inlet by the shore. No one knows why we anchor so unexpectedly. It seems that some ships turned in toward shore, and those coming after followed them blindly.

We disembark on a beach: one with little sand, just pebbles. There is no one here even to ask us why we came. . . .

Same day, evening:
– We have just razed an entire village to the ground and massacred its inhabitants.

A score of men assigned to repairing arms and armor had deserted. We discovered they had been bought off by the villagers on instructions from the Genji.

In retaliation, troops of thirty cavalrymen were sent off to surround each house and fire the thatch in the roofs with embers from a bonfire. I led my own company up to a shabby little hut on a hilltop, almost hidden by a thick *karatachi* hedge. At my command to ride around it in a circle, they began to shout in parade-ground style, but I ordered them to stay quiet and gallop fast, to make a loud noise with their hooves. Some thorny branches stuck out far enough to scratch my armor, but I hacked them off with my sword as we passed. The thunder of iron horseshoes must have stunned the people inside. The door opened a crack, and moonlight revealed the figure of an old man in a tattered nightshirt leaning halfway out.

39

We rode around the hedge several times, hearing screams as three cottages at the foot of the hill began to burn. I lined up my men:

"This shack may be deserted, but an order is an order. We must attack. Set fire to it, one of you!" The man on my extreme left raised his brand and galloped through the hedge.

The more brutal we are, the more we are hated by these defenseless people, but the less chance there is for our troops to join them. I only wish I could desert myself, and get away from these men I fight alongside.

The three cottages below the hill had been razed, leaving a half-dozen others still alight. The horsemen surrounding each one were attacking it according to their leader's preferred tactics.

Poised on the half-burned roof of one house were two naked men: one old, the other a boy younger than me. Both held stout bows and had bamboo quivers tied to their backs. Bare bodies glowed red in the glare of the flames, and the moon just behind their heads was streaked with sooty smoke. Assembling my men in a grove of evergreens, I got a good view of their brilliant archery defense.

Heedless of danger, the old man defies his attackers with classic shooting. Hardly caring that flames will soon swallow his perch, he plies his bow carefully, arrow by arrow. His self-possession in the face of death is admirable, even without the lethal wounds he is giving our cohorts.

Meanwhile the other—hardly more than a child—rests one knee on the ridge of the roof, about to take a last shaft from his quiver. But he holds his bow an inch too far out, and fire singes the string, snapping the bow forward. Still calm, he removes the quiver and slings it over his companion's shoulders; then, straddling the roof ridge to mend his bowstring, looks down as though playing with a toy. Before he can finish, he loses his balance on the shaky roof and falls. Then I notice the arrow fixed in the crown of his head.

We took five captives, one a lunatic. None of them knew where the deserters had escaped to. They swore they were telling the truth and ready to die for it, but please to spare the crazy. We led them down to the beach and beheaded them. The lunatic said nothing— only screamed like an animal. We killed him too.

– Back at camp now, but the hut on the hill still burns, raising a cloud

of black smoke into the sky. Can't sleep till I see the last of it. The men bedded down nearby talk over the night's events.
– Written down in camp the same night.

The following day:
– We have given up land routes altogether. I don't like all this sneaking about by sea. The smallest disagreement is enough to start a quarrel, making life on board unbearable. From flying at each other's throats, we go to exaggerated politeness, and at last subside into silence.
– At noon, another island, some fifteen miles around. We drop anchor in a little harbor at the southern end. They say the islanders have already sent a pledge of allegiance to the Genji. We make a pretense of throwing a party on the beach, but meanwhile split our forces into three for attack; my group stays behind to fortify the hill by digging shallow trenches at suitable points, and by constructing a palisade of bucklers, as well as a makeshift tower. The other two set off along the shoreline to east and west. However, the rugged nature of the terrain makes it impossible to follow the action from our tower.

Scouts' reports indicate the opposing force will avoid a decisive engagement.

I am standing at the top of our tower watching a red signal banner on the tip of a cape visible in the harbor. Should our adversaries approach by sea, this banner will be waved back and forth thrice. I am holding my own banner, waiting for a second report from our scouts. In the event of our east flank being routed, I am to wave it thrice, and our ships will row to the far side of the harbor to take off survivors. The commander of the west flank, a man of keen judgment, told me before he left there would be no need for it.
– The second report arrives: west flank has killed two islanders and burned seven cottages on the slope of a pine-covered hill. Weapons removed from the bodies were not made locally; their silvery arrowheads shone too bright and new not to have come from a city.

The courier who brought this news stands by me a moment, staring out to sea. He takes off his helmet to wipe the sweat from his sidelocks, apparently unwilling to descend from the tower. Perhaps he enjoys the view of our ships offshore, and the autumn colors around us. A number of wild persimmon trees grow on the slopes below, and their fruit, against the deep blue of the sea, is a glowing red. . . .

Same day, afternoon:
– I handed over my post to a samurai, by name Miyaji Kotarō.

He lives on one of a group of islands near here in a place called Mitsunoshō. After mounting the tower, he faced me and my men and dropped to one knee, bowing his head. The three men with him imitated their leader's salute. It seemed over-punctilious while we were in action, but I was pleased with the determined expression on their faces.

I could not easily judge Miyaji's age. His forehead was a network of deeply etched lines, as of an old man or one who had led a hard life. His speech was enough the product of his rustic locality to be unintelligible outside it. For all that, his voice had a lively tone that cheered me immensely.

He addressed me from the kneeling position. The gist of it, in our Rokuhara style, was:

"We four come in answer to your call for recruits, and are honored to assist you in guarding this tower. We are local men-at-arms; late last month we rode to the fortress of Sasa-no-semari just built by Seno-o and his son Muneyasu, to give them our loyal support. We are ready now to do our duty."

He stood and, with evident satisfaction, took up his position in our temporary watchtower. From behind, I judged the thickness of the bow he leaned on to be at least three times mine! His battle dress was practical: an oversize—not to say baggy—robe of dark blue cotton under armor laced in black, a sword with copper-and-gold facings, and a quiver with some of the eagle's-feather arrows we had all but used up in the day's battle. Doffing his horned helmet, he let it dangle by the cord, which turned the dragon's head on it to glare up into the sky. Its blue reptilian mouth gaped menacingly, darting forth a slim tongue to flash golden in the rays of the afternoon sun.

His men took up their positions with the same satisfaction as their respected leader. Each of the three gripped the long railing with one hand and, raising the other to his eyes almost in unison, stared off into the distance. They seemed like steady, reliable sentries. Their attire was in the last degree inadequate, the tallest having only a summer tunic held together with string, while the fat one's ordinary cloth *kosode* was tucked up in his sash at the back. The third wore a frayed corselet with a majestic-looking sword hanging from it—obviously a battle trophy. Their hunting-style or bamboo quivers, graced with a few arrows, were all as if by agreement hung with string.

– I climbed down from the watchtower to let my men rest behind their palisade, then with a single mounted escort galloped off in search of General Shigehira.

Coming down the hill, which as I say was dotted with wild persimmon trees, I was overtaken by the general's aide-de-camp, Saburōbyōé. As the muzzle of my horse fell behind the barrel of his, he raised his bow and flashed a grin. I realized he was spurring his mount to bring news of a victory. I hadn't suspected him for such a fine horseman: he was able to gallop straight down the slope into the camp and halt right in front of the general, bearing down on the stirrups and leaning low over the horse's head. I saw I was right about his news.

Officers and men around General Shigehira stepped forward in a single spontaneous motion, a solitary bow raised in their midst; the general himself only smiled. As I entered the camp, Saburōbyōé had just finished his report, and nimbly reversed his mount to ride back to the battlefield.

The horse reared up, ecstatic at returning to the field. In danger of being thrown, Saburōbyōé shortened rein and leaned over till his cuirass touched the mane, a smile of satisfaction crossing his features. When the animal regained its balance, Saburōbyōé lightly stroked its neck with his palms as if to say: enough joking. Then he threw out his chest and adjusted the reins, while his mount stretched out its neck and took off at top speed, its mane streaming in the same wind that billowed the rider's cape—a brave sight!

– As Saburōbyōé sinks from sight over the brow of the hill, the camp breaks up in confusion. One man pushes his way through the crowd; a group of people merge with another, and again divide; some men dash away, others stand where they are; all the horses tied to persimmon trees whinny and rub their necks against the trunks.

A little apart from this bustle, General Shigehira's old groom crouches by himself. With a stout black helmet on his head and a small blade in one hand, he is solemnly cutting dry grass for his master's horse. A clump of grass is left where a broken arrow sticks in the ground. Anxious to avoid the missile, he has carefully cut all around it.

Back turned on the uproar in the camp, the old man sings to himself in cracked tones as he works, elegant songs about the tears of an emperor's favorite concubine streaming endlessly down her cheeks, and of how in the Second Month—or perhaps the Third—spring would paint grass and water the same hue. His master used to sing them often, back in the capital.

– Talking of tears and sorrow, I must deal with an episode that all but ruined the élan of our clan, which had been trying to cheer up the disheartened camp with its example. Some minister of protocol's upstart young brother, acting as chamberlain on the ship carrying ladies-in-waiting, intruded himself into the main command tent where people were occupied with many items of business, to take up the general's time with an absolutely petty suggestion. It was typical that he'd have a post near the ladies where, during the battle, he could stay safely by his charges in a ship hugging the beach. At any rate, he brought a communication from one of his ladies, and facing General Shigehira delivered himself of this masterpiece:

"Clearly, our army has carried the day in this encounter. Even from the beach we can see that. My lady abbess and all the others are well pleased.

"I am to say that while success is due for the most part to the divine protection of our late Lord Kiyomori, it is in no small way a measure of the general's strategy and the skill of our soldiers. There must be some among these heroes who have authored particularly daring feats; we trust they shall be granted honor and reward. Hence, on the occasion of our victory, we wish to build a beautiful new capital on this island, with a palace on its hilltop. The lady abbess is much set on this point, and we support her idea. Seen from this vantage, the imperial residence is no more than a common hulk anchored on the beach. Historical chronicles make no mention of seagoing palaces! Let nearby manors be notified, and the construction of a proper one begin."

Thus the courtier, to which the general replied:

"The day's issue has certainly gone to us, but it is hardly decisive enough to portend the rebirth of our house! Our enemy was no more than the gentry and serfs of one island. You should understand that we built such a large-scale camp for this miserable adversary only to discover how closely Kiso Yoshinaka's forces followed us. A great army, filled with confidence, seeing such a formidable battle array, would hardly retire without attacking. Had they struck, we would have lost many in battle and by desertion. To keep losses light, I built a watchtower on top of the hill, and readied our fleet near the beach behind the camp there. Judging from today's action, the Genji van has yet to penetrate here. So far, only weapons have been sent from more civilized areas. A major upheaval must be taking place at the capital, and we should use the lull to evade our enemy. The advice you so kindly bring us from the ladies is made in good part, but I must decline to build a new palace yet!"

Heedless, the young fool chattered on of ways and means to finance construction, and of how beautiful the new capital's streets would be: he wanted them wide and straight, their flagstones quite smooth, and large dwellings for the commoners lining both sides. With such avenues and palaces, thought he, we were sure to win back the hearts and minds of the people. They would willingly embrace peace and order, in their own interest, and come to the inescapable conclusion that *our* side was the more worthy of fealty. The common people's submission and toil for us, however difficult the situation, was a mystery indeed, but they could hardly do otherwise than give us sovereignty over them.

General Shigehira answered in a low voice:

"A man who offers such disgraceful advice when our house faces ruin is too spineless even to desert. More than this kind of babbler, it is the archer on that hill who claims our love. He has a clumsy, barrel-chested look, but, as sentry of our watchtower, does his duty as best he can. That stiff, upright figure at the scene of battle fires my thoughts. . . ."

– Moving on toward evening now. After leaving the main camp and returning to my stockade, I found the men lined up waiting for me. With the oldest veteran as temporary commander, they had laid out a small camp of their own.

Same day, evening:
– I am to take my company out at first light tomorrow to reconnoiter the enemy. General Shigehira has entrusted me with five warships and a score of captured fishermen to man them.
– Getting dark: am writing this by firelight. Can see the silhouette of the emperor's big flagship out on the water, surrounded by an escort of smaller boats; their crews—gate guards from the capital—display many lights, large and small. Very foolish, especially at this time.

Miyaji Kotarō and his three retainers are attached to my company. He came up just now, with much curiosity, to watch me write in my journal. Stoked up the fire for me while reporting news of the camp. One of the senior officers has drowned himself, supposedly from being too much enamored of Pure Land teachings. I knew the man for a very learned scholar, since I'd been taught by him to recite poetry and play the flute. Young and foolish though I was in those days, he had me memorize Chinese musical theory. . . .

Next day:
– Not actually in charge of the scouting party; a tonsured samurai from Izumidera temple called Kakutan has the real command. The general is using me as a last resort against desertion. Since our retreat from the capital it has been rare for troops to desert a company led by a Heiké prince. At first, the general was going to award my post to Atsumori, the youngest son of the lord chamberlain—who gets lonely if he can't sleep next to his father in camp!

I don't mind sleeping by myself, on the ground if necessary. When I brush my palm across my cheek, I can feel the growing bristles rasp against it. Haven't cut off any heads yet, but my arrows sink into enemy shields from a good distance away.

– The monk of Izumidera never leaves my side, and confers with me before giving the most trivial orders—I suppose to make me look like a real commander in front of the men. He wears a dark blue robe under armor with black lacings; his scabbard and hilt are lacquered, the two dozen arrows in his quiver fletched in black; a lacquered cane bow is slung over his shoulder, while his helmet dangles by its cord; his pate is shaven clumsily, with scratches and tufts of hair all over it. Even a

46

poor bonze would disdain to look so slovenly! However that may be, he is master of the scholarly as well as the military arts, and well versed in etiquette. I heard there was no one in the Academy to beat him.

As we stood off from the beach, General Shigehira and other notables were on hand to see us on our way. The horses on deck neighed their farewells.

Kakutan turned to me:

"Let's get out of here. I can't stand this kind of big send-off—it's a Rokuhara custom we can do without. See that there's enough fodder for the horses, and our bulwarks are secured." He gave the signal, and my flotilla set out to sea line abreast.

Sitting next to me, my monk held his head above the bulwark on the gunwale and stared back at the beach awhile, then made himself comfortable. By the time we rounded the cape he was sound asleep. The sight of that great maladroitly shaven head wobbling back and forth over his armor made me smile more than once. And yet—let one boat slip out of line and his eyes opened quickly enough! Once, when we drew past a little island, he not only opened his eyes but glared at it suspiciously.

Our destination was none other than our own harbor of Tomonotsu, where the whole clan had stayed one night. We were going back now to look for signs of Genji movements. This was imperative for the orderly retreat of the clan's forces.

Many promontories along the shore, pointing out like offshoots from a maidenhair tree; villagers' houses along the beaches between; a few scattered thatch roofs up the slope of the hill. . . .

How I long to jump out and ride up that hill to a certain house; the girl I so impressed with my horsemanship must still be there. I want to meet her again—to gallop up the slope by myself, as before. Then I'll lead my horse into her garden and water it at the pond, as when I first met her. It is just by that pond the great pear tree grows.

Alas for private plans; our party had no time to rest. Kakutan had us anchor in the harbor and forbade anyone to disembark. If we had to go inland, he wanted every sailor tied to a deck board, or we'd be in trouble.

The new man, Miyaji Kotarō, being familiar with the topography of these parts, was Kakutan's choice for a guide, and the two went ashore together. As he left, the monk turned to me:

"If you hear a signal arrow whistle low overhead, never mind how exciting it sounds—row out to sea, fast, and get back to base. It'll mean we've sighted the Genji. Whatever happens, don't let any of your men leave the ship. Even with ten times the troops, you couldn't defeat an enemy that was too strong for Izumidera no Kakutan!"

He donned his casque, tied the cord of his visor, and gave the false moustache on it a playful fillip. Holding his bow high, he urged his steed over the side and into the water. Foam from the surf drenched his blue robe and armor. His mount kept its muzzle up till it reached the shallows, then we saw it take a big breath for the first time. Miyaji's horse didn't like being led by the other's: when it gained the beach, it dashed ahead at top speed. But Kakutan's horse was determined to outstrip it. Without a backward glance, the two riders disappeared into a grove of date trees.

– After they had gone, I called one of the sailors over and told him to fetch one of the little skiffs abandoned in the harbor. The man had nothing on but a plain helmet. When he had understood my order he took it off and slipped into the water. I inspected the helmet while he was gone, and saw it must have come from a Genji forge, as it was cast in the shape of a snail shell.

Later on, I used the skiff as a ferry and sent five men-at-arms ashore for news of our two scouts.

A little past noon, two of the men reappeared on the beach. Getting into the skiff, they rowed over to my ship. Their report follows; it was hard to avoid the conclusion that Miyaji and Kakutan were neglecting their duties:

"The five of us split up, we two to advance along the beach, following the hoofprints in the sand. After about two hundred yards, the road became gravel, then stone-paved. We lost track of the prints, but there were huts along both sides. In one doorway we saw an old man with some eye disease sitting on a blue stone. He told us two mounted men had ridden past a short while before, and gone he didn't know where. In the garden of another cottage four women were talking together. The place looked like a brothel, and the girls were in the trade, sure enough! They chaffed and flattered us to get us inside. But hoofprints in the square just south of the house led us to their honors' mounts under an old oak."

Bursting in, what should they find but our brave warriors seated cross-legged in full armor beside two women, eating and drinking! It was totally unexpected.

"Lord Kakutan was in high spirits. He made us welcome, pushed cups on us and told us to drink, but we didn't join them. The cups were funny—brown in color, wide and flat like plates. Lord Miyaji wasn't drunk: he just sat with his arms folded, looking down. The two women kept their eyes down too. It was hard to be sure, but we thought we'd seen their faces before."

After this report, the two men returned to their own ship. The skiff was next used to bring the three other scouts and an unknown woman to my ship. They reported as follows:

"We took a local woman prisoner for collaborating with the enemy. We'll explain what happened. She was with several other women of the same age, weaving straw mats inside a broken-down building. They were laughing and making fun of our army. The noise from inside made us stop and we clearly heard some slanderous remarks. She was leading the work in time to a song insulting the Heiké army by calling it 'the pinched-off tail of a lizard'!

"We thought she was a spy for the other side, so we broke in and arrested the insolent wretch. The commander must judge whether it's a capital crime. As to the whereabouts of Lord Kakutan and Lord Miyaji—we did all we could, but they weren't to be found."

Their captive stood before me, the skin of her ugly face and neck mottled with fear, but she stared straight ahead without moving. The spirit had gone out of her, and she stood there with her arms out, frozen stiff, afraid to breathe, let alone move. She was terribly skinny, like some old fleabag of a horse.

I wanted to give some recognition to the efforts of her three captors; but what could I do with the woman? I asked her some questions:

"So you think our army is like a lizard's tail, do you?"

In a broad country dialect, she apologized for her words.

"When you were taken prisoner, were you kicked or beaten by my men?"

She hadn't been kicked, but they had pinched her shoulders and chest.

"What do you know of the Genji movements? Have you noticed any rough-looking soldiers about recently?"

She had not, but forage for their advance units was ready in her area. Some of the cottagers along the beach who collaborated outright with the Genji were handling arms and provisions for them.

"You are an observant woman: I'm setting you free. Go back through the fields to your straw mats and laugh as much as you like!"

I had her put back in the skiff and ferried ashore. The moment she gained the beach, she gave a wild cry and dashed off as fast as her legs would go. The sailor who had been rowing took off after her, obviously planning to desert. But an arrow from the ship struck its fleeing target just behind the shoulder. . . .

– Late in the afternoon, a plume of smoke way down the shore. I put it to my men, and they decided a house had caught fire from carelessness. But before the first had dissolved, another appeared; it was about three-quarters of a mile nearer, still quite far. Couldn't imagine what it was— even less what it meant. There was another! This too was far away, but seemed to be a three-quarter mile nearer than the second. More columns rose into the air, keeping the same direction and spacing. They came on, in fact, right up to the harbor.

The last fire was at a big house near the foot of the hill. Just as white smoke belched from the ridge of its roof, two horsemen emerged from the date grove. It was Kakutan and Miyaji! Unable to contain myself, I beat my armor with my war-fan and yelled encouragement to them. A welcoming shout from the men drowned out my own.

The two daredevils had been setting fire to the magazines prepared by the villagers for the Genji!

They rode into the surf, and Kakutan leaped off his saddle onto the ship. Miyaji also brought his horse over, but only to shout an account of their mission:

"Reconnaissance delayed—a bit of trouble—not much to do with fighting. After a little food and drink we rode along with our eyes to the sea—saw a lot of wheel marks in the sand. That told us all we wanted to know—and sure enough we found a number of ready-made magazines. We charged them—and set them on fire."

After this simple statement, he swam his horse over to his ship.

Kakutan had a little trouble getting his mount aboard, exhausted as it was from its hard gallop. His report was even shorter:

"We took a little time. Met two Heiké women who'd run away the night our forces stayed in that village. The silly females ended up as prostitutes. Enough said."

News to make my eyes pop out! Yet there was no trace of chagrin in his face as his gaze followed the plumes of smoke trailing off into the sky. He shed his sodden armor and rested his elbows easily on the bulwark, looking every inch the plucky and daring warrior-monk he was, a man you would trust with your life. All at once I wanted to blurt out my yearning to run away. . . .

24th Day of the Ninth Month:

– From the safety of our warships, we've kept a watch on the shoreline over five days now, and still have no idea of the Genji's movements. Two men rode out of the woods yesterday, cursed us loudly, and dashed away. Otherwise no suspicious activity either in the village or on the roads leading to it. We armed ourselves and lay low behind the bulwarks, prepared for the worst, but as night came on we saw nothing more than a few women in the garden behind a house, toiling desperately to store up the harvest. The scene was peaceful, with no sign our foes were near at hand.

– Most likely the two horsemen were long-range scouts from a Genji reconnaissance unit. They came out of the grove and straight down to the beach, but turned their horses' necks ready to evade our fire and contented themselves with yelling abuse. Took up my bow all hot to reply to this, and ordered the veteran Miyaji beside me to try for a shot at the beach. I had just stood up to draw my bow, when quick as thought the two spurred their mounts in the direction they were facing and vanished among the trees. Miyaji, his left boot resting on the gunwale, leaned on his bow and smiled with chagrin, evidently impressed by their speed. Kakutan, who was also at my side, was moved to say how skillfully they handled their reins. Neither took offense at the stream of insults, which accused us of misrule ever since the Hōgen years, and of oppressing the people while we wallowed in luxury. The savage roar of their brazen voices must have been heard clearly in the village.

One of them, on a jet-black horse and holding his bow by the end to wave it in the air, wore russet-colored armor with Chinese twill lacings, and carried white-fletched arrows. Pointing the bow in our direction, he announced himself and loudly challenged us:

"You there—speak up! Heiké or Genji? Is that some kind of picnic barge you're on? Or a fishing boat? From the mountains of my northern snowbound home I come—unbeaten veteran of many battles—Gorō's my name: the son of 'Long Shot' Shigeta, a retainer of Lord Kiso's chosen, Kagemori of Nakatsu."

Needless to say, we'd never heard of this Kagemori, let alone "Long Shot" Shigeta! But Gorō, common-looking fellow though he was, rode a well-fleshed animal, and his twill lacings and gilt scabbard were those of a company commander. Such a horse and armor could be got no other way than as loot from a dead Heiké officer. The other rider sat a bay with black fetlocks and a gold-chased saddle—the only things about him that looked good. His helmet was the same red leather as his corselet, and he carried a short, thick bow. His challenge was given in an atrocious accent, so offensive to my Rokuhara-trained ear that I made little of it. He might have been a woodcutter straight from Kiso's home mountains; obviously their army is preparing a war of extermination against us. . . .

– Today a tranquil one aboard ship for a change. Kakutan complained of a headache and shaved his bald pate again. As he worked, he traded yarns of Hōgen and Heiji battles with Miyaji. Miyaji is just an old country samurai now, but when he was nineteen, during the glorious fight at the rebel emperor Sutoku's palace in the capital, he was with the force that attacked the Kasuga Avenue wing there. And at twenty-two, in the Yoshitomo affair, he took part in the assault on the Taiken Gate. When he thought of those battles, he said, his heart swelled in his chest, even now.

As for Kakutan, I am not clear how one so conversant with learned subjects and of such elegant speech could have had much experience of battle, but on finishing his toilette he took up a war-fan and spoke thus:

"With regard to skill in archery, I can't help mentioning Minamoto no Tametomo. Tametomo was our enemy, but fearless enough to quell the Lord of Darkness himself. At Sutoku's palace, one of his arrows went clear through Itōroku's cuirass and lodged in one of the pauldrons of Itōgo's armor; tough three-year knotted bamboo it was, and fletched with mountain-pheasant tails—a big powerful beggar. Another one, a turnip-shaped 'howler,' took away a good part of Ōba Heita's left knee before it punched a hole all the way through the barrel of his pony. The force was incredible. Its echo rang through the palace long after it had passed. How that awe-inspiring wail made our hearts leap! It might have risen to the blue heavens to join the music of the spheres. Well, that's the essence of war: when the clarion calls, a man must do his duty as a warrior—no more and no less!"

He emphasized the high points in his speech by pounding his knee with the war-fan. Miyaji quietly remarked that *he* had heard the sound of Tametomo's shots himself, at Emperor Sutoku's palace. The monk only grunted, "Oh did you?" and at length—whatever his source may have been—gave the story behind the arrowheads. They were a special make with ridges between the deeply scooped-out whistling holes in the bulb, and had a length of over fifteen handbreadths. But Miyaji claimed an arrow like that would break up on its way through a horse. Kakutan replied with another grunt, and fell silent. What a howl that signal arrow must have made to impress him so much!

Same day, evening:
– At Kakutan's suggestion, we lashed our five ships together. This will prevent the coolies from trying to seize one and sail off with it.
– Kakutan's gone ashore in the skiff again, with Miyaji and a captive villager to scout out the situation. The monk wore no armor as he jumped into the boat, but carried a favorite sword-lance from his early fighting days under his arm, and sang to himself as if he hadn't a care in the world:

If there be a date tree in the garden,
Let me eat of its fruit;
If there be sadness in my heart
Let me sing of it. . . .

Miyaji was fully accoutered in green-laced armor which didn't quite suit his years, the helmet with the twisted dragon's head, and a cane-bound

53

bow with two dozen eagle's-feather shafts. He made a brave figure, and obviously took his responsibilities seriously. Facing me, he went down on one knee in the style of the southern corsair of old to make a formal request for the use of my little skiff, and followed Kakutan. Their prisoner, wearing a typical Genji shell-shaped helmet, pulled on his oars and the little craft soon disappeared into the darkness. Land and sea were black as pitch. Aboard ship, my men lined the bulwarks and stared silently across to shore. Occasionally, one would change position, and the creaking of armor reminded me of how I hated the scrape of metal and its smoldering smell when I was a child. Now it rather braces me, but my attitude was slow in changing. Once I couldn't stand hearing a blade being sharpened, but it was very pleasant this morning, waking to the sound of Miyaji honing my sword-edge. Listening in a half-doze, I seemed to feel my heart beat faster. He's an expert at it, too.

– The two of them back safely after nightfall. Their "guide" had run off while they were going up to one of the houses. This was where a maidservant who'd worked for Naitō, a lieutenant in the palace guards, had hidden herself, to live among the villagers in rather disreputable circumstances. A stain on our honor, no doubt, but they got important information from her. Times change, they say, but her news of such a violent reversal of events was enough to amaze us. Kakutan gave his characteristic wry grin and commented:

"All things pass . . . esoteric prayers and incense, even the Law of our Lord Buddha, are things of a day, it seems."

He had heard that Kiso Yoshinaka was already, on the ninth of the month preceding, ceremonially invested by imperial decree with the office of protector of the capital! On the sixteenth, privilege of audience was withdrawn from all 163 members of the house of Heiké, and we were declared traitors. Also, according to the rule that not a day should pass without a reigning emperor, Prince Takahira has acceded to the throne. He is to be called Gotoba.

As to our being declared traitors, I talked with the monk till nearly dawn about it. He insisted we had made a serious mistake in not escorting Ex-Emperor Goshirakawa away with us. However, I'd say the refusal of the warrior-monks of Nara and Mt. Hiei to rally to the imperial banner is one of the chief causes of the present disorder. It must have shocked Kakutan how easily his brothers-in-faith turned to serve the devil—it was a proud boast that he was one of the few who'd done his duty.

– Miyaji Kotarō sat quietly beside Kakutan all this time, listening to our conversation until we had finished. It is his habit, whenever I write in my journal, to build the beacon fire up so that I can see. I am writing this by the same light this evening.

26th Day of the Ninth Month:

– "Fish-scale" clouds in the sky today, but the sea is calm. Kakutan and Miyaji just back with more news from Naitō's former maid. Rumor has it Kiso is planning a punitive expedition to the West Country. However, Ex-Emperor Goshirakawa is not likely to give him leave, by any special decree, to do so. Kiso wanted to put up the Hokuriku prince against Goshirakawa's candidate for the throne, but this was unacceptable. A naturally violent man, he doesn't take kindly to opposition; his behavior exceeds all bounds of arrogance and brutality. His troops, now out of provisions, have taken to looting—even tearing up green rice shoots to feed their horses! The mood of the capital (more especially of the elders of the court) is not tranquil. Kiso's popularity has never been lower. They say the ex-emperor is ready to give the Fujiwara of the north, who are close to the old regents, a mandate to oust Kiso entirely.

When I heard this last, I breathed a sigh of relief. If we could only take advantage of unrest in Kyōto, and rebuild our strength in the West Country in the interim! But Kakutan only looked up at the sky:

"Ah, well . . . those clouds seem to be laughing at all our fine theories, including the one about the Latter Days of the Law."

If his interpretation is right, the Genji of Kamakura may well risk all on a single throw and accept the ex-emperor's mandate themselves. A civil war among the Genji clan would soon bring a literal Hell on earth!

– Their informant also said that on the sixteenth last, when offices and titles were stripped from 163 of us, Chief Councillor Tokitada, his cousin the director of the storehouse, and his son the governor of Sanuki were spared disgrace. These three were asked to help bring back the putative

55

emperor, little Antoku, safely to the capital with the sacred jewel, sword, and mirror. All very well, but couldn't they at least have made the gesture of resigning their official titles? If this news is true, we other Heiké will also suffer from the taint of treachery. Sanuki consulted his own safety by retiring to the plains and mountains near Saga and Ōhara, where he sallies forth daily to the hunt with his white falcon on his arm, after making a show of having abandoned the world. But some traveler in the know had watched him at first hand, and left the news of his dissipations with Naitō's maid this very morning!

This pilgrim, it seems, had hidden from the world himself. He thought such a course prudent at times, but in the usual circumstances, he explained to our maid, it was shameful for a man to do so. She kept him talking till dawn and eventually got the most important news of all: some members of the clan have actually reached Dazaifu, our defense headquarters in Kyūshū! Together with Harada, Kikuchi, Usuki, Hetsugi, Matsura, and others from Kyūshū they are building a temporary capital. I must now face the fact that my squadron has lost sight of the main body. When we fled the capital, we sailed too far and too fast along the shore from Fukuhara to maintain contact with the others. Yet as a commander of a unit of the rear guard, under the new lieutenant general, Sukemori, I must now lead my ships out to reconnoiter the enemy's movements as ordered.

We must sail for Kyūshū without delay. I have conferred with Kakutan and made plans to leave with the tide tonight.

Same day, evening:
– Advancing line astern. Miyaji Kotarō's ship is in the van for his knowledge of local tides, while mine is at the tail end. I write this by the cheerless light of the watch fire in the hold. Kakutan has taken several men forward as lookouts, to keep us in line with the others.
– Just before we sail, I lead a party ashore for food, water, and firewood. Taking only one man for escort, I pay a brief visit to the house of the pear tree. It was here I met that girl when I was billeted in the village with our larger force. Later she came to me on a beach below the cliffs, saying little, only stroking the hilt of my sword. Seeing her hair

done in Rokuhara fashion, I was grateful for the care she had taken with her grooming. But what makes me happiest is that I inspired affection in someone outside my family and class.

Today I stay a little while in the garden of her house. It is not yet dark, but the door is shut tight without a sign of anyone within. The branches of the pear tree have been roughly broken off short and left to wither; the ground beneath is covered with rotting fruit. There is no mistaking the signs of a deserted house. I feel an impulse to inquire where she has gone, but I realize how useless it is. My guard goes around to the back door and emerges again to stand staring back and forth from the broken branches to my face. It is the custom of our family at such times to improvise some poignant verse, as he well knows. But I say nothing. . . .
– Our vessel now caught in the narrows, its hull seeming to split the current in two. Kakutan comes aft to warn us we might be sailing into a kind of cul-de-sac, which they call Mouthless Strait in these parts. He claims that once, while accompanying Bishop Eryō on his pilgrimage to Itsukushima Shrine, he saw hundreds of dolphins swimming in the water hereabouts.
– I go forward to look at the sea. The moon is not yet out, but I can see beaches on shore and an island hemming in our destination. More than ten days ago, as part of General Shigehira's army, we camped behind the steep crown of that island. Then, after sending us on reconnaissance, he left us without warning and sailed for Kyūshū. Kakutan heard as much last night from the maidservant—but what a feeling of being abandoned!

27th Day of the Ninth Month:
– Dropped anchor just before dawn at a place called Tamanoura. The bulky mass of an island lies squarely in the harbor's mouth. Here also, the sea becomes as narrow as a river, just as it did at Mouthless Strait.

A-single night-fishing dory lay near the rocky island. Kakutan ordered some soldiers to bring the fisherman aboard. They went forward, threw a grapple over the dory, and hauled it close enough for one to jump aboard and boost the man up to our decks. The poor devil was expecting rough treatment: as they were hoisting him up he clasped his hands together, babbling pleas for mercy and so on. Kakutan told the men to go easy, but they still manhandled him a little, as soldiers will. With a guffaw at the sight, the monk conducted our prize to me and cross-examined him as to name and domicile, as well as the situation in Tamanoura.

Still unaware he was not a prisoner, the fellow lay prone before us like a frog, not daring to look up. He was trembling with fear. A man of sturdy build, he wore only a quilted navy-blue singlet reaching down to his hips. When he stood up his groin was exposed, with a coil of fresh straw tied about his private parts. His extravagant obeisance must have been to conceal his nakedness!

He stated he was twenty-nine years old, by name Saba, son of the widow Sazaé who lived on the rocky shore at Samba, some way along from the harbor. He was master of the dory we had seized. His speech was antiquated but pleasant, in the manner of an old song; I couldn't understand more than half of it. Nevertheless, as I listened I was able to follow most of Kakutan's conversation with him. It seemed the area around the town had been recently annexed to the demesne of Minamoto no Yukiié, ally of Kiso Yoshinaka. At the foot of the mountain behind the harbor, Yukiié's family and retainers had entrenched themselves in a ravine stronghold. It was an ideal position, with the open sea in front, an inlet on one side, a gully on the other, and a good view from the mountain behind.

The mountain was a high one, like Fuji in shape, flowing down to the sea and seeming to loom right over our decks. Despite a bright moon rising, its silhouette remained dark, and I was just able to make out the pale white shape of the great bare crag on the summit.

To put Saba more at ease, Kakutan presented him with a jacket dyed with oak bark. For the first time, the man raised his head and a pleased expression invaded his face, but when asked if Yukiié's men were not plundering, rioting rascals, he collapsed into his former frog-like posture. Of course they plunder and riot, he admitted. Yet worse by far were the pirates from Kyūshū that had begun to raid the area recently. Many cargo bottoms plying the straits between here and the coast of Shikoku had been confiscated in the name of self-appointed "governors" like Ki no Michisuké.

I exchanged glances with Kakutan. Michisuké was deputy governor of Nagato in my father, the vice-councillor's, name. I remembered his manly face from my childhood, certainly not as one belonging to a pirate. Father had described him as an able administrator and a cultivated man.

Kakutan kept his own counsel and went on to ask Saba what news there was of Emperor Antoku's temporary headquarters. The fisherman knew nothing. After some questions on shipping routes in those waters, he was ordered back to his dory.

– Dawn broke, at last. Kakutan went forward to signal the lead ship a course that would conceal our little fleet behind the island. Miyaji hoisted sail and, as the others followed suit, led us out of the harbor and off to the west at full speed.

There were many cottages on the shore we were leaving and, farther off on the slopes of the mountain behind the harbor, a five-tiered pagoda and some temple buildings. But on the steep side of the smaller island across the strait, wrapped in water like a sash, there wasn't a house to be seen. A long narrow spit stretched from its western end, and off the tip, as if it had rolled there, was a solitary islet. Rounding this, we reached the south side and open sea, hidden from land by the bulk of the island. Kakutan again signaled Miyaji. We moored our ships where water lapped right against the rocks, lining the five of them up and lashing them together, bow and stern.

– Kakutan suggested we keep a little way off from the men and beckoned Miyaji over for a three-man conference. What the man Saba had told us was hearsay no doubt, but might well be a true reflection of the common understanding. Whatever the case, our leaders had to retake Kyōto sometime, and to that end would have to gather their courage and win the heart of the West Country. The commander in chief, Munemori, my close relative and a former minister of state, must surely have realized this. If the fisherman spoke true, the clan had already left its Kyūshū headquarters to storm the capital. In any case, something very much out of the ordinary was transpiring at our imperial camp; I .wanted to hasten there and find out what. I asked Kakutan's opinion.

Serious though our discussion was, he gave his loud laugh. As he saw it, our army had been *chased* from Kyūshū. Something was undoubtedly going on at the imperial camp; but most likely it was running in search of a safe place! Since they were already hard-pressed, better for our squadron to stay on the offensive and secure the nearby coastline.

Miyaji Kotarō thought we should first ascertain the truth of our intelligence. He came from the local gentry of the island nearby called Innoshima. Having a deep grasp of the geography of the area as well as the character and dialect of its people, he was the obvious choice for a reconnaissance. To do it properly, he asked for one ship; he would not deprive us of fighting men, but content himself with miscellaneous ratings. Kakutan bowed to him humbly and asked, "May I go along as your aide?" The other man's surprise showed on his face, but with his hand on his buckler he gave courteous assent. "I would be honored."

I approved Miyaji's plan, offering a second ship to the monk for his own use. He accepted gladly, and further proposed that Miyaji take his three faithful followers with him. The old samurai had brought only these when he first rode into our camp. All had hereditary obligations to his house, and were likely picked men. Shabby in their accouterments, yes— but in strength and capability worth many times their actual number. – From all these reports, Kakutan concluded a battle was coming that could not be avoided. He inspected his men's arms minutely, and garbed himself in the most dashing manner possible. Armor laced in black was worn over a robe with green arabesques on a blue ground; a casque with five segments to its neck guard, surmounted with horns, was tied tightly to his head; and his weapons were an awesome-looking sword, arrows fletched in black and white, and a lacquered strongbow. This attire suited his dignity wonderfully well, in no way resembling that of the usual down-at-heels bonze.

Miyaji had his off-green armor and the helmet with the twisted dragon's head, two dozen eagle's-feather arrows, and cane-bound bow. He had brought new black armor as well, but felt more comfortable in the worn green outfit. No doubt its youthful color reminded him of former days, and of brave deeds in fighting at the capital.

Miyaji took his own three stalwarts, ten men-at-arms, and ten coolies aboard ship with him. Kakutan took about the same aboard his own, and the two made sail with the latter leading. I saw the monk, bow under arm, take up a position in the bows of his ship. Beside him squatted an orderly to hold his favorite red-handled sword-lance, like a banner urging them on. . . .

– I kept the remaining three vessels lashed together and started the locals we'd captured repairing the rudders and replacing deck boards the horses had damaged by planing new ones out of broken bucklers. Of the four prisoners, one knew smithing, another carpentry, and the other two were bow-makers. Kakutan had taken them in anticipation of our eventual need of craftsmen. They were, I think, resigned to their lot; without waiting for orders, the four had begun shaving broken boards down to make torches for our watch fires. Then they fished until nightfall for something to make oil from. Perhaps fishing was a consolation too. Our smith was best of all: before the others even got one, he could hook four fine black bream. I noticed the hook he used; it was an anchor-shaped affair of his own making. The line, he told me, was woven from the tails of dead horses.

I had stabled three horses aboard ship, but they wasted away until they died and we had to throw their carcasses into the sea. The smith must at some time or other have removed their tails. I watched all three of them go overboard, but so deft was he I never saw him picking the tails. The white hair in the line he must have got from my own mount, Kisaragi. He was a favorite of mine I took from the stable when we left Rokuhara. When Kisaragi went over the gunwale, the heavy splash as he hit the water made my heart contract. I kept his saddle and stirrups as mementos, and later gave them to the smith as a reward for his work. He sent word through my soldiers he wished to forge a special set of two dozen arrowheads for me.

He had admired the saddle extravagantly. Its metal fittings, worked in pure silver, were made by the capital's finest craftsman, Yasumitsu of Kamo. My father got the idea from that line of Po Chü-i's about a silver saddle on a white horse. Once, at the height of our prosperity, I put the saddle on Kisaragi to roam the woods around Uzumasa with a falcon on my wrist—a popular pastime at Rokuhara and my father's particular hobby. How passionately we were devoted to such "pastimes". . . . Ah, Rokuhara! The father and mother of us all—how sweet your memory!

Same day, evening:
– Wrote letters to my cousin Kiyomuné, a captain of the palace guards, and my little niece Rokudai. Didn't know where to send them, so after reading them over I tore them up.

28th Day of the Ninth Month:
– Kakutan and Miyaji still not back. Ordered a soldier called Jirōji— nicknamed "Seven-Leagues"—to climb the mountain on the island for a look. He carried provisions for three days but returned the same afternoon, running down the slope at top speed, almost sliding from crag to crag. He stood over on the beach, breathing hard as he shouted his report: he had just seen the two ships in the distance, making sail away from us. But half a dozen enemy vessels were chasing them!

Seven-Leagues came aboard and told me what he'd seen in detail. He had gone right to the peak—rather a high one—and looked all around, at both sea and shore. In the harbor we had left at dawn yesterday he saw six ships appear, hoist sail, and come out line astern. After them came our scouts' ships, straight as arrows, the two matching the movements of the six point for point. But when the two overtook them and changed course, the six came after them directly. Our companions were vastly outnumbered. . . . Brave Kakutan! Old warhorse Miyaji! How it would gall them to retreat. Perhaps they would engage, counting on skillful maneuver and sea room to decoy the enemy away. There was no doubt the two ships were ours. Seven-Leagues was confident of his long-range vision—there could be no mistake. He drew a deep breath when he had finished his report.

Feeling the urgency of sending reinforcements, I asked in what direction our companions sailed. Seven-Leagues looked down in confusion. He knew only that their ships were sailing southward this morning. He had come down the mountain as fast as he could to deliver his news, but lost his way en route and landed on a strange beach.

He tried walking along the coast in search of the ships, but steep cliffs thrusting into the water at both ends prevented him continuing along the shore and keeping the mountaintop in sight. He was forced to retrace his steps, climbing the peak once again to get back to camp.

I assigned another man, Koyata, the troublesome task of staying at

the summit to keep a lookout till nightfall. I told Seven-Leagues to retire and rest. A little crestfallen, he turned over his provisions—still
untouched—to Koyata. Feeling a little sorry for him, I said he could ac-
company Koyata if he wished; that cheered him up, and he went off
with the other.

– Our smith was already forging my arrowheads under the rock shelter
down at the beach. With help from the two bow-makers, he made his
hammer ring from morning to night with his blacksmith's work. The
sketch he made showed my special arrows to be basically the carved
cherry-blossom type, only with heads filed to a slightly longer, spear-like
shape. With my immature skill at archery, I suspect I won't always hit
my mark with that type of head. My left arm is weaker than my right.

Our carpenter was felling pines up the mountain. This man also had
a sketch for me, of something like a thatched hut. We might have to
leave this beach tomorrow, but already he was leveling off ground under
an old oak at the foot of a cliff. He had put up a branch of the sacred
sakaki to placate the spirits of the earth he was building on. Once in
a while, he would hum an air in time to his woodcutting, and as I
watched his absorbed, contented figure I was seized with envy. . . .

– As evening drew on, a solitary eagle lighted on a pine tree atop one
high cliff. The coolies jumped to their feet, shouting. Speaking for the
bow-makers, one of them asked our best archer, Ni no Suenari, to bring
down the bird. Its wings had just the right kind of feathers for my precious
arrows. Cursing them all into silence, Suenari quickly pulled on a protective glove and strung his cane-bound bow, then took two arrows and
jumped down to the beach. He stared up at his target, which sat right
at the tip of the tree, nocked an arrow, and raised his bow. Slowly, draw-
ing it fully back, he let go with a twang! The eagle spread its wings for
flight, but instead fell straight down the cliff face. Suenari deftly nocked
a second shaft. But the bird struck the sand pierced to the heart and
Suenari, looking a little awkward, had to release the string and lower his
bow.

Craftsmen and coolies clapped their hands in delight, and one ran up
to the foot of the cliff. He picked up the eagle and faced me from a
distance, raising it for me to see. He seemed to be asking what I meant
to do with it. I waved my hand, and he extracted the bloodstained arrow

and took the bird over to the bow-makers. Suenari is such a sure marksman that when my eagle's-feather arrows are done, I think I'll give him a set.

– Suenari was back aboard wringing out the hem of his tunic, which had got wet on the beach, when the men gave another shout. Off to the south, to the right of a large island, were several ships under full sail. I counted eight in all, lit up by the setting sun. But the two in the lead could be none other than Kakutan and Miyaji's! The six following seemed to be deep-draft cargo boats. All eight were still formed line astern, keeping a regular order together. The soldiers and coolies were now calling to one another: "Those two are ours! It's Captain Kakutan!" I wasn't sure, but I thought I saw in the bow of the lead ship a man in armor who could have been my monk. I immediately gave orders for a single smoke signal to be made. It was the hour of evening calm, and as I had hoped, the line of smoke rose straight into the sky. I stared across the water in an agony of suspense until from the lead ship's stern came an answering line of smoke. Then the wind scattered it low over the sea.

To make certain, I sent two more smoke signals . . . again the answer came. I felt inexpressible relief, almost crying in my joy. The eight vessels then disappeared, one by one, behind another island to the right.

– When the sun had set, I called for a samurai by name Fukasu, noted for his loud voice. Told him our two captains had captured half a dozen of the enemy's supply ships. I bade him shout this news to the men as loudly as he could. When he had understood, he went forward to the bow and bellowed out in his famous voice:

"Oyez! Oyez! Hearken to the news of our camp. Two of our ships have this day taken a round half-dozen of the enemy's supply ships. Tomorrow we'll grab ten of their men-o'-war like swatting flies! We'll take a fort in the morning and another at night. Our enemy's the foulest under Heaven, but we'll send 'em there before us! Oyez! Oyez! To arms!"

The soldiers and coolies—even the prisoners—raised their voices in the rousing battle cry used by our navy in its rare moments of triumph.

Same day, evening:
– All the men looking well pleased. Since we fled the capital we've had no occasion for cheering until today.

– Assembled several men-at-arms with Fukasu and Suenari to have a little parley and spin a few stories about Kakutan's exploit. We were just laughing about Seven-Leagues' absurd report when he appeared, accompanied by Koyata. Noticing the mood of elation in the ship, they lost no time in getting the story out of the crew. The two now stood in front of me, great fatigue showing on their faces. They reported simply; around nightfall they had sighted our companions' ships ahead of the enemy. Realizing how wrongheaded his first guess was, Seven-Leagues looked mortified.

– The wind has come up, bringing a slight drizzle. It's a long time since I heard the sound of rain. . . .

29th Day of the Ninth Month:

– Our two heroes returned at noon. The six supply ships were full of provisions, and five more large ones had new recruits aboard. Both Kakutan and Miyaji have covered themselves with glory. Those left behind welcomed their triumphant forces with round after round of spontaneous cheers.

The two commanders, however, had looks of disquiet on their faces. Miyaji came aboard my ship to give a hurried salute, tell me he was giving orders for a general muster of troops and disposition of the fleet, and leave. Kakutan took me a little aside from the men around us and made an equally brief report.

The spoils of their foray were six bottoms loaded with provisions and 146 men distributed among five others. Of these, forty-two were Miyaji's own retainers, and another sixty those of Michiyasu, chieftain of the island of Yugeshima. Michiyasu himself had sworn allegiance to our house and come along with all his retainers. The remainder were followers of Matsunaga, the "lay bonze" of Hashirijima; he had luckily been away, so Miyaji managed to spirit away at least forty-four of his men. The provisions had been stolen from granaries at the fortress of Tamanoura, now in Minamoto no Yukiié's territory. They hoped to lure the other country samurai into submission by rifling his storerooms first to impress them with our wealth . . . but Kakutan would rather I not record this as his battle in our chronicle.

He explained to me hurriedly, "You see, Miyaji Kotarō's valor and initiative made a daring raid seem almost routine," and went on to report rumors of how the clan was faring in Kyūshū. If these were true, our people's situation couldn't have been more pitiable.

Presently in Kyūshū were the armies of Harada, Kikuchi, Usuki, Hetsugi, and Matsura. These were at first allied with the Heiké in welcoming the young emperor and establishing his camp in Dazaifu to protect him there. However, in the Second Month of this year the banners of Harada and others were raised against us. Fujiwara Yoritsuné, son of Lord High Marshal Yorisuké, had left Kyōto on a punitive expedition against them and was still in Kyūshū as deputy governor. But although he was our deputy, he had opposed the clan's entry into the defense headquarters there, citing the ex-emperor's decree. Then, allying himself with a bandit chief of uncertain pedigree but considerable power, he had conspired with Usuki, Hetsugi, and Matsura, and with their allied armies attacked the Kyūshū base. All at once our people found upwards of thirty thousand horse hard upon them. Harada and Kikuchi's group offered battle in defense of the young emperor while the Heiké clan escorted our sovereign to a safe place—at top speed! At this point, a heavy fall of rain allowed the litter bearers to desert, leaving no one to carry the August Palanquin. His Imperial Highness was placed in a sedan chair and respectfully requested to travel to Hakozaki. There the Heiké, again following their emperor, occupied the stronghold, but on the rumor of a hostile approach abandoned it. Taking small boats and hugging the shore from one bay to another, they came to a place called Yanagigaura, in the province of Buzen. That was on the tenth of this month. The wanderers must have been sore pierced by the chill winds of that bay: on the night of the thirteenth, under a bright moon, Lt. General of the Left Kiyotsuné took a boat and, steadily reciting prayers the while, consigned himself to the waves.

But let Kiyotsuné drown himself how he will, and let his aide commemorate him with mournful notes on his flute—none of this would soften the thirty thousand cavalry coming against them. If the Heiké stayed at Yanagigaura, at Yanagigaura they would be attacked. Should they flee to Usa, then Usa would be their grave. Knowing this full well, Ki no Michisuké, the deputy governor of Nagato, put together a fleet to bring the young emperor across to Yashima in Shikoku. Altogether he had assembled five hundred vessels to ferry the whole clan over. I wonder if the half-naked fisherman we grilled at Tamanoura the other day didn't give us the other side of this story.

Kakutan tightened his helmet strap for no particular reason—he must have forgotten to take it off—and insisted we hasten to weigh anchor. The slightest delay meant losing a chance to secure the Inland Sea for our own side.

Struggling to hold back my tears, I donned my armor and gilt-mounted sword. Then I fixed my quiver with the two dozen eagle's-feather shafts high on my shoulder and picked out the heaviest of my three bows. Kakutan inspected me from front and back, right and left, arranged my helmet to give me a proper bullnecked, stiff-shouldered look, and thrust a baton into my sash at the correct angle.

Ready for action, the two of us left the ship. Our army was drawn up on the beach in four columns. My personal troops faced me on the left, and diagonally behind them, with Miyaji Kotarō in the lead, stood a line of fifty-odd men mostly in black armor. A little distance away from them on the right, a force of no more than sixty formed a third column. Kakutan whispered that these were Michiyasu's. Behind them, at the same angle as Miyaji's column, stood a fourth line of forty troops. In the lead, wearing dark blue armor, was the man who had so skillfully downed my eagle yesterday, Suenari. Probably made their leader at Miyaji's insistence. Without being told, I knew they were the former retainers of Matsunaga of Hashirijima, recruited by Miyaji.

Guided by Kakutan, I mounted a great flat-topped boulder which had rolled down to the edge of the beach. Seen from this height, our army formed a crescent-shaped, or Crane's-Wing, battle formation. Miyaji, who was so used to commanding a pirate navy himself, would have felt exposed by any other arrangement.

My five orderlies at first stood outside the formation. But by the time I was ready to inspect the whole force from atop my boulder, they were standing below me. One of them appeared on my boulder carrying a campstool; he set it down and retired again.

Kakutan squatted down next to it, knees apart, bow thrust under arm. Taking my place on the stool with aplomb, I solemnly removed the baton from my sash and held it upright on my knee. At the same moment, my army raised their bows as one man and saluted me with a cheer.

In this position I issued the order to break camp, but took the opportunity to make them a short speech of encouragement:

"Hear me, one and all! Our honor is defended by a gallant company, and under the high skies of autumn our horses call out their defiance. The hour of battle for our just cause is come! The enemy harried our beloved young emperor by far sea roads to Kyūshū. Now they have driven him as far as Yashima. This enemy must be obliterated!

"My loyal officers and men are gathered here before me. Who are they? First: the peerless Yugé Michiyasu and his party. Second: the brave men of Matsunaga. Third: Miyaji Kotarō and his party. Last: the retainers of myself, Taira no Tomoakira, scion of the clan Heiké. Trusting in the gods, let us advance and secure the brocade banner for the emperor and our cause!"

At the close of my address, the men cheered me once more. Their voices rang with determination to serve me faithfully unto death.

Same day, evening:
– Now on the island of Ōmishima. Lost a dozen men in battle today, but left a score of enemy dead and gained 102 recruits from the other side! I intend to press on and take the islands up to Yashima one by one.
– I'm so tired. Want to go to bed.

29th Day of the First Month (1184):
– Established a beachhead in the Bay of Suma before daybreak. I've gazed at the peak of Mt. Tekkai before—there are still traces of snow on it. Here at Fukuhara when it was the capital, Father taught me to revere it as a holy mountain. Once I even saw a crane alight on its slope.
– My family's old house lies in ruins. Nothing remains but a few cracked tiles; even the foundation is falling to pieces. The Miscanthus Pavilion and the charred ruins of the two-storied Hall of Balconies have been ploughed into wheat fields. The skeleton of the beachside villa has become part of a poor peasant's lean-to.
– After lashing the ten hulls of my fleet together, billeted my men in townspeople's cottages. Have rigorously forbidden looting or womanizing to please Kakutan. He has disguised himself as a plain bonze and

gone among the people as a spy; he didn't return till after dark. His information is, the ceremony of changing the name of the era has been consummated in the capital, and the period is now officially "Genryaku." Also, on the twenty-first just past, Kiso Yoshinaka's army, which had terrorized the capital for so long, was dealt such a blow by Kamakura Genji forces that it fell to pieces and was destroyed. Kakutan heard the details of this battle from a tramp on the road. There were six thousand horse in the Kamakura army, which split into two corps before assailing the capital. One of them, led by Minamoto no Yoritomo's brother Noriyori, attacked Seta, and the other under Yoshitsuné stormed Uji. Kiso's army had only two thousand cavalry, and these likewise were divided between Uji and Seta. The former group was routed first and forced across the river by Yoshitsuné. He at once divided his men into several columns and pressed the attack. Knowing the battle was lost, Kiso took refuge in the palace and demanded audience, with the ex-emperor's approval. By this time, the Kamakura army was besieging Kobata, Hachijō, and Fushimi. Kiso had to abandon any idea of an audience, and thundered out of the palace with the three hundred survivors of Uji to meet the Kamakura army on the riverbank at Rokujō. Here they were again routed, and in order to join the Seta force, crossed the Nagasaka Pass by way of Awataguchi and rode down into Ōmi. The Kamakura Genji then burst into the inner city of Kyōto. Yoshitsuné proceeded directly to the palace gates, where he called out a report to the throne from horseback:

"I humbly present myself, the younger brother and envoy of Minamoto no Yoritomo. Obeying the august instructions, I have broken through the Uji road and now stand at His Imperial Majesty's service!"

Deigning to be impressed, the ex-emperor came out to the middle gate to favor the dismounted victor with his regard. Yoshitsuné was accompanied by five doughty warriors; the emperor asked the name, age, and birthplace of each "gentleman from the east," and was kind enough to comment on their looks, saying they seemed like men to be trusted for a fight!

Meanwhile, Kiso's Captain Kanehira, guarding the crossing at Seta, was being forced back over the Kugo Shallows by Noriyori. Kanehira had only five hundred horse, and the larger force prevailing, he was vanquished. On his retreat to Ōtsu, he fell in with the defeated Kiso and a pitiful half-dozen survivors in a field near Awazu. By now it was nearing sunset. Kanehira raised his standard from the dust, so to speak, and from forest and ditch came riding a steady trickle of Kiso's remnants—enough at length to make up a force of four hundred. It may well have been Kiso's intention to flee along the North Road, but Noriyori had already surrounded him. He was fiercely assailed till the 400 were reduced to 300; the 300 became 200; the 200 only a hundred, and then a mere score. After a running battle, Kiso's followers were whittled down to one—Captain Kanehira. Kiso was obviously ready to kill himself right there. With the few shafts remaining in his quiver, Kanehira covered their retreat to the pine grove of Awazu. His last arrow gone, he halted to face the host of their pursuers, and stood up in the stirrups to shout:

"Men of the east—hear me! I am a man of Shinano, son of Imai Kanetō. Since leaving my country I have fought many battles, never to be defeated. I am Kanehira of the Imai family, the milk brother of Kiso Yoshinaka. My name is well known even to your lord in Kamakura. Strike down this Kanehira and you will earn your master's praise."

At that moment, Kiso, ready to dismount from his horse, turned to face in Kanehira's direction. Instantly an arrow struck his helmet—a fatal wound. He sagged until the front of his helmet rubbed the pommel of his saddle; a Kamakura trooper cantered up to the body and took his head. Kanehira, still on his horse, disemboweled himself, then put the point of his sword in his mouth and fell headlong from the saddle. He lay there with the blade showing through the back of his neck. That day, Kiso was wearing a robe of red brocade and armor laced with Chinese twill, as well as a horned helmet with a five-plated neck guard, and a sword with gilt mountings. His steed was a powerful animal from the Kiso hills named Gray Devil.

The ends of Kiso and Kanehira were no doubt already known both within and without the city of Kyōto. Miyaji, who went abroad as a spy a little after Kakutan, confirmed the news in all important particulars. – A large party of reinforcements from Yashima came ashore after dark. They brought the imperial barge and its escorting boats with them. However, on the off chance of a night attack by the enemy, His Imperial Highness remains aboard. His barge lies at anchor hard by the beach at Wada, to be his seagoing residence outside the capital. His guards gather wood on the beach, but light no campfires for fear of attracting enemy eyes. My own billet is at present beside Miyaji Kotarō's fire. I again write this record by its light. Kakutan sleeps with his back to it.

30th Day of the First Month:

– That is, the thirtieth day, First Month, of the first year of the so-called Genryaku period. But I want to write "thirtieth day of the First Month, third year of Juei," and keep writing it—third year of Juei—there!

Furiously busy from early morning, building a fort to defend our camp. Villagers and coolies hauling logs and boulders for the walls and lumber from the mountains for the gate-towers.

Our fort is to be narrow along the north–south axis, and spread out east to west, according to the plan we have from General Shigehira. It was decided to put our frontline gate at the point facing Ikuta Wood in the east, and build another fort to our rear at Ichinotani in the west. There are three leagues between these points. Headquarters will be at Fukuhara. The building plan provides for a watchtower here and palisades for the troops at Minatogawa, Itayado, and Suma. Other palisades and buckler fences will stretch from the foothills of the mountains in the north, down to the shoals in the south.

An imperial camp is being laid out at Ichinotani, and our rear guard will hold the whole line to the west of there. This extends our battle array as far as the bays of Muro, Takasago, and Akashi! The valley of Ichinotani is 500 yards long, 40 yards wide, and 120 yards from the beach to its mouth. Between Ichinotani and Ninotani stretches a bluff 320 yards long, along which the clan has built its fortifications. The imperial camp is surrounded by earthworks taking up an estimated forty square yards. Trees have been transplanted to the front of the young emperor Antoku's pavilion as a windbreak, with pipes laid down to water the garden, all together making suitable accommodation for the August Personage.
– Kakutan remarks that, on the map at least, our defenses look formidable.

"Construction should be finished as soon as possible," he adds, gazing off into the distance. "Yoshitsuné is still in the capital, but he'll be rounding up the stragglers of Kiso Yoshinaka's army as fast as he can.

71

The heads of every last one'll be up on Jail's Gate inside a day. Never you mind his recent victories; Yoshitsuné will finish his business post-haste and come down to settle with the Heiké clan once and for all. He's already requested a decree from Ex-Emperor Goshirakawa to outlaw us. It's common knowledge the Imperial Council met at the palace on the evening of the twenty-first, and granted it.

"And today the ex-emperor delivers himself of another confidential decree to us: a negotiator is to be sent on the eighth of next month—until then, positively no fighting! The Genji commanders have all been personally notified, it says, and it's hoped that the Heiké will consider returning to the capital in company with the young emperor—and his sacred regalia, of course. Another ruse by the palace advisers to get the regalia back to Kyōto! We must finish building our forts without delay. Yoshitsuné is legendary for his speed, and must already be breaking camp."

The warrior-monk's opinions were disquieting enough, but he voiced them in an oddly elated tone, staring off into the sky all the while.

– Two of Miyaji's work crew injured today: one pinned under a piece of lumber and breaking a bone in his shoulder (all his own fault); the other disinclined to work and about to run away until spotted by an overseer, who broke his arm. Both middle-aged levies from Minatogawa, their lives fortunately not in danger. After swearing to report for work directly they were healed, they left for their homes with long faces. In any case, most of the townspeople in Minatogawa and Fukuhara have already disappeared. When I awoke this morning, the family of ten in the house where I'm staying was gone, young and old. Kakutan remarks that the common people have an infallible sense of how the world is going, and says it's a sure sign the Genji will attack soon. Be that as it may, our people half believe in the ex-emperor's assurances, and make no special effort to hurry the defenses.

– Late in the afternoon a fleet of forty sail under the governor of Noto anchored by the beach at Wada. Apparently left Yashima on the ninth and fought a series of engagements among the islands of the Inland Sea. Says he was able to negotiate a truce with the pirate bands on Shiaku and Kurushima on the way. This news spread through the camp like wildfire and Kakutan was very pleased; now we'll have the freedom of the waters west of Akashi Bay. I have it from Miyaji that the pirates of Shiaku are much to be feared. He should know: up to last year, he was the chief of a band of pirates himself, operating from Innoshima in Bingo—until they made common cause with the clan, that is, and General Shigehira gave me command of them. As tough and honest as they come, the old corsair is a loyal ally and a master seaman, and has since become the favorite crony of Kakutan, who is of the same superior mettle.

All the same, he's not too proud to stoke the flames up for me as I write. Kakutan is sleepily tracing characters from the sutras in the ashes of the fire. Whole lines form and vanish under his stick—what a memory! Must be thinking of his younger days at the Academy, when he was the star student. . . .

1st Day of the Second Month:
– The watchtower at the Fukuhara fort is completed. An array of red Heiké banners wave from its crown, and the general's old groom is up there, too, beating a drum and from time to time giving voice to our war cry.
– Sat on a pile of lumber below the cliff all day, watching Miyaji direct his workers. He's had evergreen trees transplanted behind the palisade and an abatis set up outside it. Looks like a cross between a cheval-de-frise and an ornamental hedge. Lt. General Sukemori himself, on a tour of inspection, said it wasn't badly done. But my father, who had come on a tour only moments later, remarked that the time we spent on our "ornamental hedge" might better have been used to dig a trench at the base of the cliff. I'm not surprised they can't even agree on the best type of defense, since my father advocates storming the capital directly, while the lieutenant general wants to build and defend a full-scale fort. A man with the cool blood of Shigemori, the statesman, in his veins will always avoid battle if he can. . . .
– The palisade facing Ikuta Wood is seven parts done. Our rear-line fortification toward Ichinotani, however, is not even one-third complete.
– Kakutan off early this morning to scale Mt. Takatori with the workmen getting wood for the abatis. He was full of jokes, complaining that our regulation against looting and wenching was killing him with

boredom. He's forgetting the regulation was made at his own suggestion! – After dark Miyaji, Kakutan, and I sat around the fire talking of the Kamakura Genji soldiers. Lacking their experience, I was content merely to listen and learn. Kakutan estimated the enemy horse at five thousand; Miyaji thought two thousand more likely. The eastern forces numbered over six thousand when they first invaded the area, and destroyed Kiso Yoshinaka's two thousand in a single day. But the easterners must have had heavy casualties themselves. It was debatable how many of these had mended, but the monk's guess was over double that of Miyaji's. This was proof of the former's high regard for Yoshitsuné's strategy and daring. Moreover, since the affrays of Uji and Seta, there had been no new draft of recruits for his army. Yoshitsuné must be a general supreme in wisdom and bravery to earn such an accolade from Kakutan. He went on to say:

"It makes not a particle of difference to Yoshitsuné if he has the sacred regalia or not. He thirsts for vengeance, and has but one thought for the Heiké clan: can he or can he not crush us? Now—he's thinking—is the time to avenge his dead father, Yoshitomo. He burns with fighting spirit; cares nothing for obstacles, natural or man-made. His elder brother Yoritomo's purpose is only to secure the Kantō Plain above Kamakura, but Yoshitsuné, with or without his brother's orders, imperial fiat or no imperial fiat, has resolved to exterminate the Heiké!"

Kakutan finished by remarking that Yoshitsuné's vengefulness showed a classic determination to "wipe away all shame," and explained the Chinese origin of this phrase to Miyaji. The latter remembered hearing it before; it seems it's becoming a catchphrase.

The monk used no honorific expressions and talked simply of "Yoshitsuné," but Miyaji went on using the more respectful term "honorable cadet." Yet his opinion of the "honorable cadet" is by no means as high. To him, the fount of Genji valor dried up with the passing of Minamoto no Tametomo and Genta the Wicked. After joining the Heiké army during the Hōgen and Heiji affairs, he had seen heavy street fighting by the river and the Taiken Gate. What he saw of Tametomo and Genta made a deep impression on him:

"Whatever you think of the honorable cadet," says he, "he's not the equal of the great departed—Tametomo and Genta. Besides, the clan now has armies from the five central provinces and environs, as well as from those by the Inland Sea—a total of over twenty-seven thousand men!"

Poor Miyaji believes all our allies to be as staunchly loyal as he.

2nd Day of the Second Month:
– To Tamba today with my father and the general of the left to reconnoiter the road. From Ichinotani we rode through Shioya, Shimohata, Taibata, Miki, Ono, and on to Mikusa. Part of the eastern Genji forces will almost certainly come around by this route. We had an escort of two score or so, and did some fast riding at times. Didn't notice till we got past Shioya that Seven-Leagues was running behind my horse! He likes nothing better than dashing along with a group of horsemen. Probably he'd been waiting for his chance, but it must have been torture at that pace. Even so, he found time to pick branches of blossoms from roadside plum trees to take back as presents—and without scattering petals, too!

The Tamba High Road is extremely narrow. Just before the village of Taibata, it takes to the mountains and narrows still more. There it becomes a rough track burrowed out by rivulets—more like a ditch, next to impossible to negotiate on horseback and a natural death trap in the event of an ambuscade.

At Shimohata on the way home, darkness overtook us, and we sent Seven-Leagues on ahead. Back at camp, I find Kakutan warming himself by the fire and construing a book on tactics for Miyaji. Most likely the scroll had been brought out at the latter's earnest entreaty. At Yashima the good monk never did this without being asked many times, protesting that his listener already had the military classics by heart. No doubt Miyaji wanted to hear favorite passages intoned in the impressive voice of a man he revered.

The old warrior is listening in a properly respectful posture. Kakutan, back to the fire with scroll unwound before him, declaims the same section over and over. Both appear to consider it a weighty utterance.

I have heard
That in battle

It is best to be swift
And strike fiercely.
I never saw
A skillful general linger
On his way to war.
I have heard
That in battle . . .

Miyaji silently faces in my direction, adjusts his position, and salutes me, all in silence. Kakutan lays his scroll aside and bows solemnly. I describe the Tamba High Road to them: its narrowness, the shape of its mountain track, and so on. Typically, the monk already knows more about the state of the roads than I do.

I listen awhile to the sound of the waves, quiet and restful. . . .

Kakutan's habit is always to turn his back to the fire before falling asleep. Miyaji then takes over stoking the fire for me. A little while ago, a branch of plum brought by Seven-Leagues recalled to Kakutan a Chinese poem he enjoyed reciting in his youth, called simply "Miscellaneous Stanzas":

I have watched the winter plum blossoming,
Again heard the song of the birds.
With a feeling of melancholy
I gaze on the spring grass
And, facing the palace steps,
Picture them covered with weeds.

The author of this poem was the T'ang writer Wang Wei, whose sobriquet was Mo-Chieh, man of T'ai-yuan. The subject, of course, is the coming of spring.

Same day (postscript):
– Rumors of a Genji attack early tomorrow morning. But not likely for two or three more days. In every camp, soldiers, coolies, and locals have been put to emergency preparations. The commander in chief has assigned the defense of Mikusa Hill, on the Tamba High Road, to the governor of Noto, the bravest and most respected man in the clan. For some

unknown reason, Noto declined this duty—perhaps to save his energies for the coming naval battle. Lt. General Sukemori departed for Mikusa in his place.

– Should the attack actually come tomorrow morning, a signal will be made from that direction with a conch or bamboo tube, and all forces are to muster at the sound of the big drum.

3rd Day of the Second Month:

– The rumor of a coming attack turned out to be groundless, probably started by Yoshitsuné himself. He made it look as if he had left Kyōto, to forestall any siege on our part. By now he has really left the capital and is force-marching his way here.

A council of war just past noon, at a temporary camp. Kakutan gave me some good advice to pass on to my father.

"We're waiting for the eastern Genji army to attack our front line at Ikuta Wood and our reserves at Ichinotani. But they'll have to detour around us to reach the rear, and once out of Kyōto they can't avoid taking the Tamba High Road. From Kameoka they'll reach Sonobé, go through Sasayama and over Mikusa Hill, and from Harima Province they must come south through Inamino. While they're making this long detour, we can strike north from Ikuta Wood and storm the capital!

"The easterners have only so many troops, which they must divide between our front and rear lines—making their van, it goes without saying, even weaker. Why sit here and wait for them? If the army in our rear is Yoshitsuné's own, we'll have the chance of a lifetime. Our twenty-odd thousand will make short work of Noriyori's force in front, then we can march on the capital. There'll be a triumphal return to the city we all remember in our dreams. Now is the time to go back to Rokuhara, the mother and father of us all!"

I conveyed his words to my father in what I hope was the same stirring fashion. After searching my face keenly, Father praised me with tears in his eyes, saying I'd become a splendid, manly fellow. Later, I was told the council of war had made the decision to stay within our defenses. Shigemori's sons—Sukemori and company—had voted down Noto's and my father's exhortations.

Kakutan greatly disappointed; has spoken not a word since. Can't help feeling the same way myself. Miyaji still more downcast. He went off to his "ornamental hedge" at the base of the cliff a while ago. The monk sleeps as always, his back to the fire. . . .

4th Day of the Second Month:
– Today an anniversary: our revered ancestor and clan patriarch, Taira no Kiyomori, died on this date. Buddhist ceremonies held on board the imperial flagship, anchored near Wada beach—I heard prayer bells ringing all over the camp. Everyone talks of the coming attack, supposedly delayed three days. This is, after all, our memorial day, and Yoshitsuné would judge it a great crime to interrupt our religious observances—or so it is believed. As for tomorrow, the western direction is forbidden, and the day after is unlucky! In reality, the story about our enemy's religious scruples may have been spread by Yoshitsuné himself. He is most likely on his way this moment, to catch us with defenses unfinished. And given that he spread false rumors to smooth his way out of Kyōto, he is almost certainly detouring by the Tamba road as I write.
– After attending ceremonies on board the imperial flagship, I paid a call on Father, still in my court attire. I felt in my bones the enemy was nearly on us, and I wanted to say goodbye to him and my younger brothers. I found him prepared for the worst. It was difficult for me to speak for the tears choking me. Seeing me in this state made my two brothers, only ten and eleven years of age, burst out crying themselves. Father thought it unbecoming for me to give way to emotion while dressed for the court. He tried to rebuke me, saying that, young as I was, I was the governor of Musashi—then he too was overcome. Mother was in attendance on the emperor in his flagship; I returned to my post without seeing her.
– As I was changing from my court robes, I noticed the sword Kakutan had worn until this morning thrown down by my armor. A folded strip of white silk was tied around the hilt. The message—in a skillful hand—said he had deserted our fort, but if I felt inclined I could pay a visit to his hideout any time! He intended going to Tanada on the Ikuno road. In a postscript, he left me his cherished *hirumaki* sword "to show in a small way my regard for my lord."

Kakutan had risen that morning in the blackest of moods. Noto was tied to the defense of Mikusa Hill, and no other Heiké general was now willing to strike north from Ikuta Wood. His sympathy with the clan's fate must have run out. Taking advantage of the flurry over the ceremonies, he had calmly shouldered the red-handled sword-lance and strolled out of camp. . . .

5th Day of the Second Month:
– Kakutan's desertion yesterday left me thunderstruck—and Miyaji Kotarō, who looks on him as his mentor, took it just as hard. Him I trusted above any of my retainers, officers or men, for a superiority none of us ever questioned. His studies in Chinese philosophy and astrology had given him an unexampled understanding of the world's affairs, and made him a loyal and effective servant of our clan in its struggle to quench the fires of war. Such a faithful spirit deserves the highest praise.

Yet desertion was a serious violation of martial law, and I couldn't get out of reporting him to headquarters. I instructed Miyaji to take them the evidence of Kakutan's flight. This was the long *hirumaki* sword wrapped with silver and wisteria cord he always wore, and the piece of silk on which he had written the note. Miyaji duly took them away, but returned shortly with a face like death. He turned to me silently with a bow of respect and in silence retired to one corner to bow again. He knelt on the floor like a peasant convicted of some unforgivable crime, placed hands on knees, and lowered his head almost as far as it would go. It was clear to me as daylight he had concealed the evidence of his revered comrade-in-arms' offense. Though he had pretended to go to one of the forts at Ikuta Wood or Ichinotani, Miyaji was by nature inept at falsehood and came back in too short a time. From our quarters to Ikuta and back was five and a half miles and to Ichinotani and back, six. He had further forgotten to make it seem he was leaving on his horse! I didn't crossexamine him, however, merely thanking him for his trouble and tacitly approving what he had done. Among the golden words passed on to me by Kakutan was: know when it is better to "look without seeing." About a general's proper practice with his men, he would say: "Don't admonish them lightly, don't kill their spirit, and never let them lose their initiative!"
– Perhaps it would have been better not to tell Miyaji about Kakutan's

flight. If it becomes known to my immediate retainers, it is bound to have a bad effect on the fighting spirit of my entire command. Seven-Leagues has already sniffed out something of the affair. He not only runs faster than anyone else, but is uncommonly shrewd at ferreting out secrets. This morning, before dawn, he burst into my quarters to report that Lord Kakutan was wandering back to our lines. He had seen him calmly pass the watch fires at the gate of Ichinotani Fort carrying his sword-lance, and hurried to tell us. Without thinking, I shouted for joy and gave him one of my old tunics, as I often do, but admonished him nonetheless: "You are a ranker," I scolded; "it isn't your place to interfere with a great captain," and chased him out the door.

Taking Miyaji with me, I climb a hill to the charred husk of an old villa and wait for Kakutan to appear, ill at ease to be face-to-face with him so soon. . . . Formal to the last, Miyaji falls to his knees beside me, as if his friend were coming from a thousand leagues away . . . as the west lightens, morning mists roll up the beach over the ruins of a seaside villa and along the old road to Fukuhara . . . from the foot of our hill, a dim figure emerges—it's Kakutan swinging along with his sword-lance as a staff . . . forgetting my unease I raise my war-fan and wave . . . Miyaji raises his and calls out the battle cry we used at sea . . . an answering cry comes, not from the monk, but from a soldiers' bivouac in the burned-out villa nearby . . . from the depths of the mist another battle cry can be heard . . . responses come from other ruined buildings, the Miscanthus Pavilion and the Hall of Balconies . . . then from the watchtower floating high above the fog comes the beat of a big drum to silence these random cries . . . bom, bom, bom, bom—the same sound that spurred on the construction of the fort . . . we dash down the hill to be lost in the mist, and lead our errant comrade back to shelter.

It was no whim that brought him back to us. On his way out it occurred to him the abatis around my company's area was still a weak spot, and resolutely he turned back to warn us. We had erected it at a distance from the base of the cliff to guard against attack from above. In this, Miyaji had but followed the plans issued by General Shigehira. Kakutan now tells us we should push it right up against the cliff.

Unfortunately, we have run out of time. Last night's intelligence confirmed that the enemy is planning to attack tomorrow at noon. Kakutan must have known that with the decisive hour upon us, there was no margin for reconstructing defenses. It was obviously to set his mind at rest he came back, if only to give this last word of advice.

All Miyaji could do was muster the townsfolk and my irregulars and dig a ditch between our entanglement and the cliff. This would nail the enemy horse right against its base.

– Kakutan stayed closeted with us all day writing down a record of all that has happened to us since leaving the capital—a project he has talked about starting before. It shall be called "A Journal of the Juei Period," and bids fair to be a bulky production: he hopes not to be killed before finishing it! "But now that I have happily come back to you," he says, "I don't mind getting a taste of this Yoshitsuné's mettle."

– As usual I write by firelight. Miyaji squats down to keep it from going out, with Kakutan sitting cross-legged and brush in hand beside him, absorbed in the writing of his journal. A peaceful hearthside scene; you wouldn't think there was a war on. . . .

6th Day of the Second Month:

– Battle at Mikusa Hill last night. Yoshitsuné launched a surprise attack using oxen with sharp blades on their horns and burning brands on their tails, inflicting heavy casualties. Mikusa Hill lies on the border between Tamba and Harima, and the camp there was responsible for defending the slopes. It was annihilated. The commander, Lt. General Sukemori, Major General Arimori, and Tadafusa, the chamberlain of Tango, broke and retreated as far as Takasago Bay in Harima, from where they were driven right into the boats waiting to take them off the beach to Yashima. The only general officer to make it back to the main camp at Ichinotani was the governor of Bitchū. It was only when he and his commander of foot gave the alarm that headquarters noticed a battle was lost.

The news was brought to our camp in the morning by my orderly Seven-Leagues, who returned again at noon with a detailed report of the debacle. After leaving the capital, the Genji covered the two days' ride in one and advanced as far as the eastern approach to Mikusa Hill, establishing their base at a place called Onobara. Their commander was of course Yoshitsuné, his officers Inagé, Toi and his son Magotarō, Sahara, Kumagai, Hangai, and the rest—all names to conjure with. Our own forces were encamped on the access road to Mikusa Hill. The Genji had crossed it after nightfall and pressed their surprise attack around midnight. They had swept down the hill with a fierce battle cry, setting fire to wood and field and farmhouse, and fallen en masse onto our forces. There might have been ten thousand of them; our own people, numbering at most two thousand, were scattered in no time. Noto, however, who had the rear guard on the slope, was able to hold the Nagasaka Pass with the help of the governor of Echizen.

Seven-Leagues could give no other details, but a courier arrived from the fort at Ichinotani to fill them in. The defenses on the slope had definitely been breached, but Noto, with Echizen and ten thousand men, was dug in at Nagasaka Pass. The governors of Satsuma, Tajima, and Wakasa had arrived at the west gate of Ichinotani in the rear with twenty thousand more. My father and General Shigehira were riding to the front line in Ikuta Wood with five hundred horse. The other commanders had split up to establish camps at Fukuhara and Minatogawa. The two hundred men in my own company, together with those of Master of Stables Yukimori still at Yumeno, had been ordered to Ikuta as reinforcements.

I had already been to the great shrine at Yumeno to officiate at ceremonies of departure, resolving to guard our defenses at the cliff base with my life. Such were the orders of Vice-Councillor Tomomori—my father, that is—who commanded our van. However, since the instructions seemed conflicting, I sent Yugé off to headquarters posthaste.

Eager to carry out his mission of honor, he vaulted onto his rust-and-cream mount and sped out of camp. He passed the courier's fawn-colored animal and even overtook a horseman in red armor heading in the same direction. He flashed into the forest like an arrow just as Kakutan came out of it. The monk had galloped around to the rear to reconnoiter the Genji positions. Such had ever been his habit before a battle, but a samurai who enjoyed doing reconnaissance by himself was indeed a rare one!

He found the enemy pressing upon our rear in three parties. They had about a thousand cavalry in a grove of pines at Shimohata, two hundred-odd in one at Taibata, and another hundred at Shioya—thirteen hundred in all. The estimate of ten thousand that Seven-Leagues had relayed was an erroneous one made by the governor of Bitchū under duress of the debacle at Mikusa Hill. Kakutan's chestnut had been grazed in the haunch by a spent arrow. He smeared the wound with the animal's drool and switched his saddle to a reserve mount, Phoenix.

– Yugé back after an hour. His report is that headquarters first directed me and my company to the west gate at Ichinotani. But if the courier's message had directed us to Ikuta, said they, then we must go to Ikuta. On the other hand, if my father, commanding at Ikuta, had ordered us to stay and die with our backs to the cliff then die we must! Yugé is well pleased, basking in the glory of an audience not only with an aide-de-camp but with General Shigehira himself.

All kinds of theories in the air at headquarters, but no clear strategy. Kakutan's opinion:

"They're afraid your father will leave Ikuta Wood on his own and strike for the capital. We've only five hundred horse at Ikuta to throw against Noriyori's huge army, while against Yoshitsuné's paltry thirteen hundred at Ichinotani we're reserving a massive force of thirty thousand! This crazy distribution can only mean one thing—HQ intend to sacrifice Ikuta and hole themselves up in the fort at Ichinotani—and if that fails, they'll take to the boats and skulk at Yashima."

He again deplores our failure to seize the initiative at Ikuta. "A concentrated push in that direction," he says, "was what Yoshitsuné had most to fear. The greater part of the Genji army is there, poised for an assault on Ikuta Wood. As for Yoshitsuné himself, with only thirteen hundred troops at his command, he can do little more than harass our rear and keep his eyes skinned for opportunities.

"As I see it, any man who calls himself a soldier has one choice in war: either to besiege the capital, or use it as a base to mount an attack on some other place. In the present state of affairs, any other action is futile. Now even the former course is closed to us," he sighs. "We should have seized our chance while Yoshitsuné was force-marching his troops down the Tamba road."

Miyaji Kotarō very much inclines to this opinion but, unlike the author of it, keeps his composure. The doughty old warrior would like nothing better than to stand before the commander in chief's horse and scatter

83

his enemies to the four winds. The stiffer the fight, the better! As broth that has cooled is no longer broth, so a battle that goes easily is no kind of battle.

– It is long since we kept such a vigilant night watch. Seven-Leagues tells us that from the peak of Mt. Hachibusé one can see the watch fires of Yoshitsuné's troops, far off among the pines of Shioya, Taibata, and Shimohata. He has indeed divided his forces three ways, as Kakutan was able to observe. His vanguard in front of us has established a main camp at Koyano.

A clammy wind this evening, and a depressing gloom seems to fill the air. Kakutan has come closer to the fire to write his "Juei Journal." Miyaji is here too, with his whetstone of a strange pale blue atop his buckler, sharpening my sword. This whetstone is a prize taken from the camp of Yoshitomo's routed army, when he was a youngster serving in the Heiji wars.

The men sleep quietly all around us, on makeshift pillows of helm and quiver. By the entanglements, our sentries stand in full armor.
– Written by firelight.

7th Day of the Second Month:
– Imperial decree from the capital yesterday. Ex-Emperor Goshirakawa's secretary has sent a letter to our commander in chief, Taira no Munemori. This states that an emissary from the palace is to arrive tomorrow, on the eighth. The ex-emperor desires a truce to last until his man's return to the capital. The Genji have been notified of his will, and we are expected to inform our own troops and refrain from hostilities.

Conferences in the main fort at Ichinotani began at dawn, and the commanders of each camp received instructions to demobilize their troops. But while our men were taking off their armor, Yoshitsuné launched a treacherous attack in force on the beach at Wada, where the imperial flagship rode at anchor. Our side had respected the decree by retiring to our ships and leaving the young emperor protected only by the court ladies and a few bodyguards. The Genji naturally took advantage of this by rowing out to the flagship—an outrage! Our navy did all they could to safeguard His Imperial Majesty from these marauders, but early this morning while it was still dark the Genji assaulted our lines, penetrating as far as the west gate of Ichinotani. And at Ikuta Wood, a pirate captain and his henchmen stormed the fort's gate, breached our entanglements, and did great damage.

– My man Seven-Leagues dashed out of camp this morning when he heard the drum give the call to arms, and hasn't returned. No sign of the enemy yet. Only the sound of the watchtower drums and tocsins has reached us, and it drowns out distant battle cries. Miyaji and, later, Yugé each took a party of reinforcements to Ikuta Wood. Aside from myself, Kakutan, Fukasu, Suenari, and a few others, about fifty men left in camp.

– The battle must have been fierce. Only two of Miyaji's men, the islanders Tōta and Tōji, made it back to camp. They say both Miyaji and Yugé have been killed, fighting in front of my father's horse.

Tōta had an arrow through his cheek, at an angle luckily, but still can't talk. Tōji with a sword cut in his shoulder, but spoke rather of Miyaji's final moments. When the old corsair and Yugé got to Ikuta, the Genji were already inside its defenses and on the rampage. The enemy commander, one Kajiwara, with a squadron of a hundred cavalry, gave the battle cry. Then all two thousand of the Genji forces took it up, including those inside the fort. When at last they fell silent, Kajiwara stood up in his stirrups and declared:

"Do none of you know whom you see before you? I am the mighty Kajiwara Heiza of Sagami, descended in the fifth generation from Gongorō Kagemasa of Kamakura, a warrior renowned as the equal of a thousand men! At the age of sixteen, my ancestor rode in the van of Hachiman-tarō Yoshiié to the siege of Kanazawa Castle in Dewa! An arrow in his left eye only made him charge the harder, and plucking it out, he shot down the enemy marksman with his own shaft!"

His armor was of red leather, his cloak the color of peach, and he straddled a great fawn-colored horse. The defenders, awed by his vigor, had given way before him left and right, when my own Miyaji Kotarō advanced to their head, stood up in his stirrups, and shouted back:

"I am known as a samurai, under Izumidera no Kakutan his aide, of the illustrious lord of Musashi, Taira no Tomoakira, already famous at the age of sixteen. Thrice last winter, at Mukaijima in Bingo, at Ōmi-shima in Iyo, and again at Mizushima in Bitchū, he was victorious in battle. Look upon Miyaji Kotarō, sixty years of age, born on Innoshima in the province of Bingo, and never once defeated . . . men of Genji! Did you not hear of the imperial decree yesterday? You and your Kajiwara are nothing but cowardly bandits—come and try this Miyaji Kotarō!"

That mighty voice, forged by years of command of ships of war, could be heard far and near, inside the fort and out. Brandishing his sword he rode forward to face Kajiwara. At this point an enemy arrow took him in the left knee, and just as he was recovering his balance Kajiwara's big, well-fed charger caught his own full in the chest. As Miyaji's horse recoiled from the shock, Kajiwara struck straight downward with his sword. Miyaji tried a stab inside his adversary's helmet. But Kajiwara landed his second blow on Miyaji's casque and, as he was slipping from the saddle, severed his head with the third.

Such was Tōji's description of the sad death of Miyaji Kotarō. As for Yugé, he was cut down by a couple of common ruffians from Musashi. Father was still in the fort when Yugé fell, but was later lost sight of. He must have retreated and made his way onto one of the waiting ships. . . .

– Our own sector forgotten by both sides. The struggle in Ikuta Wood commenced about four this morning, our people were routed at some hour unknown to us, and the end may have come a little after eight. Tōta and Tōji must have ridden away from the fight at eight exactly: the shadow of our entanglement had just reached the ditch below the cliff. I saw several deer from the mountains flying along the top of the cliff, and a fawn slipped and fell straight down into our ditch. It scrambled out and stood for a moment on the mound of turned-up earth, shiver-ing. The men were about to take it alive when it bounded off in the direction of the Yumeno encampment.

It must have been little before eight when the drums in all the towers stopped beating.

Kakutan seems to have lost every bit of his martial ardor. When Miya-ji and Yugé were leaving, he did his best to stop them. When Tōta and Tōji fled back to us, he insisted we make for the boats at once. He had waited to savor Yoshitsuné's brilliant strategy long enough; he saw no reason now why we should go on holding this isolated outpost. Under the circumstances, we could do little more than retreat out of the enemy's reach, anyway.

– Took the fifty men left to me, and two wounded, and broke camp. With Kakutan, who knew of a good escape route, at our head, we galloped away as fast as our horses would carry us. The foot soldiers, shouldering their sword-lances, were left to follow as best they could. Kakutan followed the Genji's advancing hoofprints through the Yumeno camp and around the foot of Mt. Egé, then along the pine-wooded left bank of the River Karumo until we came to its mouth. It was while we were passing Mt. Egé that I got my first glimpse of the Kamakura Genji warriors. Ten of their horsemen had dismounted by a farmhouse and were leaning on their bows conferring on some matter.

Kakutan engaged them before they could climb into their saddles, and quicker than the eye could follow, his old red sword-lance had sent five heads flying! Holding the haft well back, he approached his quarry obliquely and swung the blade in great circles. What an elegant display of skill! As we rode away, I looked behind and saw my troop of fifty had dwindled to thirty. The wounded Tōta and Tōji were no longer with us. Had I not seen it myself, I would never have believed the animal ferocity and bottomless reserves of courage these Kamakura men had.

We found our slain comrades strewn around the gate-towers of the fort by Mt. Egé. They had fallen everywhere in the woods along the River Karumo, leaving swords and lances and banners on the ground about them. There was no doubt of the terrific speed and concentration of the Genji assault.

As we came out by the river mouth, more of our dead—men in full armor—lay on the ground. Fortunately, about a dozen boats had been left high and dry by the ebb tide. There were many more in the offing, far and near, carrying Heiké standards out to sea without order or system. Yoshitsuné's main army was decimating our forces at Ichinotani, and from the beach we could see a cloud of their white flags fluttering in the distance. . . .

We left our horses on the sand and manhandled one of the abandoned boats into the water. By this time, the thirty who had trailed behind us were reduced by half, the others felled by long-range shots as we passed the Mt. Egé watchtower. Among those with us was Seven-Leagues, who had left our camp under the cliff earlier that morning. He had been up the watchtower at Mt. Egé until now, observing the tide of battle. From there he had seen everything, and wept, as he told us, at the rout of Ichinotani. From there he took in Kakutan's feat of beheading five Genji, and saw me draw my sword and wound some others. A dozen of his companions had been the targets of long-range arrows and he saw half of them fall. The earlier defeat made it impossible for him to get down, so he had been hiding behind the big drum since morning. Others who braved danger and descended were killed.

One boat was all we could get into the water. My men were used to handling sail but had only got one up when, as if at a signal, thirty enemy horse appeared from nowhere. We had to take cover behind the bucklers we found ready on board. Our mounts had all scattered except for my Lightcloud and Kakutan's Phoenix, who swam faithfully after the boat. Taking our eyes off the horses, the monk and I watched the sails far out to sea. Then I looked back and saw all thirty of the enemy crossing swords in a melee with those of our troops who couldn't get off the beach. Lightcloud reached water shallow enough to stand in, then, as if shying at something, broke into a gallop and dashed along the strand toward the west, where the white Genji banners were heading. Phoenix followed in the same direction.

– A mile out to sea, we made for the southwest. From there we spotted over fifty vessels flying red Heiké standards being launched, each trying to be first away from Ichinotani. The fort there had fallen; we could tell by the white banners now waving over it. Back on the beach, white was driving red before it like a row of tumbling pieces on a chessboard and slowly extinguishing it. Another thirty-odd red-bannered ships were rowing offshore.

When the last trace of red had disappeared from the fortifications, a long line of white snaked out through the gates and lunged toward the west along the high road from Shioya to Akashi, where the stragglers of our defeated army were fleeing.

The ships off Ichinotani headed for the open sea without formation.

A large one of light draft made in our direction. As it was about to pass, Kakutan went forward and raised his hand to shout:

"That vessel looks like Lord Moritoshi of Etchū's. Am I correct? This is Izumidera no Kakutan speaking, a company commander of no special rank, left on watch below the cliff. Is Lord Moritoshi alive and well?"

A man in scarlet armor came to the bow of the other ship and called back:

"This is indeed the vessel of Lord Moritoshi of Etchū. Alas, our poor master is no longer among the living. He met his end in bitter combat, back in the valley."

Kakutan once more raised his voice:

"Heaven no longer sends us justice! . . . Humble soldier as I am, may I offer my condolence on Lord Moritoshi's death?"

Another armored warrior appeared on the bow:

"As all of you know, my lord was strong enough for fifty men. In the fight at Ichinotani a short while ago, he captured Inomata no Koheiroku, a soldier famous for his physical strength. He was about to wring the man's neck when Koheiroku, only pretending to submit, ran my lord through from behind. Nowhere—even in the world to come—shall he escape our hatred!"

The big ship passed and floated on.

Next a red-lacquered craft, with turned-up bow and stern, drew near. A man with red leather lacings on his armor stood forward to address us. I knew him for a company commander in the retinue of Lord Chamberlain Tsunemori, by name Shinohara:

"The ships out there seem to be those that came to reinforce our front line. Can we assume the general in command, Vice-Councillor Tomomori, has crossed over safely? I, Shinohara no Yukiyasu, after witnessing the last moments of Atsumori, youngest son of Taira no Tsunemori, am filled with sadness."

Kakutan rejoined:

"I believe the vice-councillor got across. But I am only Izumidera no Kakutan, a samurai who wasn't given a chance to view the battle in person."

The red-lacquered vessel drifted away. Others came up and went past one after another, each time adding more names to those lost in battle. Narimori, who had no title, the governor of Echigo, and many others of each family in the clan had been killed or wounded—not to mention General Shigehira, taken alive by the enemy.

All this time, our craft was overtaking others. In this way we learned who fell at Ikuta Wood: among them, the governor of Satsuma, the governor of Echizen, the still untitled Tsunetoshi, and others who were killed by Minamoto no Noriyori; then those who had fallen at the hand of the enemy commander Yasuda Yoshisada, such as the governors of Tajima and Bitchū. At one point we came abaft a boat with torn and ragged sail, from which rose the question:

"Is it true the lord of Musashi, commanding the camp below the cliff, was killed?..."

Kakutan was able to deny this absolutely, for "the lord of Musashi" was none other than myself!

The house of Lord Chamberlain Tsunemori was by far the worst off. The three brothers, Tsunemasa, Tsunetoshi, and Atsumori, had all been killed. Atsumori was only one year older than me. He had married when he was installed in office, and at the end of last year had a child born to him, but he was destined not to realize his hopes—a great tragedy.

Now, at sunset, we are off Awaji. Can't even think of bed tonight. Since Kakutan, with his usual composure, is using the firelight to write his journal, I have retired amidships to write my own. But Miyaji, who used to look after the fire for me, is no longer in this world. . . .

The imperial flagship is protected by more than ten other craft. It is being taken straight to Yashima.

19th Day of the Second Month:
– We separated from the others yesterday, including the flagship, and had to overcome adverse winds to reach our present safe harbor: a place called Kojima, situated in Bizen, which out at sea looks like an island but is in fact a narrow peninsula. During our flight from Ichinotani, Kakutan kept advising me to secure it. He explained its strategic position, dominating the Sanyō High Road, which made it the only place feasible to prepare for the advance of Yoshitsuné's army to the straits of Shimonoseki.

From Kojima we can cut Yoshitsuné's supply line to the straits by denying him any shipping. The clan is sure to be driven from Yashima and forced on to Kyūshū, but we can at least fight a rearguard action here. To launch our independent mission, I had to tell the chief councillor our rudder was damaged, and then abruptly changed course.

I had by now acquired great respect for Kakutan's uncanny resourcefulness. Without actually reading the stars, he foresaw future events with ease—an ability that had yet to fail him. I resolved to place all my trust in him, and build a fort at the exact position he recommended.

– Today Kakutan took twenty men and paid a visit to the estate of one Kusuné, head of the local family of Ōhashi. He galloped by the house without stopping, straight through the village nearby, and back to camp. This show of force was effective, and Kusuné soon showed up in simple attire without crests, leading a score of coolies bearing tribute. The monk suggested my campstool be placed by a great oak tree, so that I could sit with my back to its trunk and, with him beside me as "chamberlain," give a formal audience. To either side I lined up Fukasu, Suenari, Yugé's brother Jūrō, and other of my men. Sufficient, we thought, to impress a country samurai with my rank and prestige.

Kusuné advanced to within a few paces, knelt upon his buckler, and prostrated himself in the attitude of a prisoner of war. His bearers stood outside our stockade of green bamboo, their backs laden with offerings. Acting as my representative, Kakutan put some questions to him; Fukasu assumed the role of secretary, writing down Kusuné's replies one by one. Kakutan spoke loudly enough for the coolies outside to hear. He began by paying judicious compliment to our visitor's self-esteem:

"You are Kusuné of the celebrated clan Ōhashi? We know that name well in the capital. Your house must be of venerable lineage."

·Kusuné raised his head and spoke with dignity, more or less in the style of Rokuhara:

"For this humble rustic to be granted audience with Your Excellency is a high honor for his house and its posterity. My family is not from an old line—still less descended from Heiké or Genji—but is proud to offer its respects to your noble clan."

Kakutan gave a guffaw in his easy way:

"Well, well—you are a man of modesty. What age have you attained this year?"

"I beg pardon; I ought to have told you. Your humble servant is no more than twenty-three this year. When I received word that you were established here, I felt I should come immediately and present these offerings."

The monk nodded vigorously at this, and again speaking loudly for the bearers' benefit:

"You are young, but an excellent fellow. You know how to pay your respects. We do not come to despoil you, only to station our troops. You may go about your affairs in complete safety. We are here solely for the just cause of ridding the emperor of certain barbarous traitors from the east who have dared to rebel against him."

At this point, Kusuné removed a five-inch square of thin wood from his sleeve and, still kneeling, pushed it in my direction. Suenari stood up to take it and place it in front of Kakutan. It was a list of presents, written in a skillful hand. The monk faced me to read aloud:

We offer the following, with the greatest respect.

Item: Clear well water from Kakigasaki of this demesne.

Item: Rice and millet from the granaries of Ōhashi no Kusuné.

Item: Ten rolls of white silk.

Item: Ten pounds of gold from Kanemaru Village.

Item: Two and a half hundredweight of iron sand from the River Takahashi.

Item: Three boats.

Our humble offerings complete as listed above, and respectfully presented to the Heiké general on bended knee.

Ōhashi no Kusuné

When Kakutan had finished, he ordered our men to lay their bucklers out before me for Kusuné's bearers to place the presents on. As the two of us had arranged previously, I removed the spare sword I was wearing for the occasion and offered it to Kusuné as a sign of my favor. When Kakutan took it to him, he received it on both sleeves in Rokuhara fashion and quietly conveyed his gratitude by lowering his head over it. At such refined behavior, I exchanged glances with Kakutan and nodded in approval. Kusuné made another obeisance before standing up, and yet again before retiring, and I noticed the curious resemblance his features bore to the young Atsumori's—he who had fallen at Ichinotani.

Atsumori was known to our family as a most prepossessing young nobleman, who accepted his reputation gracefully. He would wear light makeup even when leaving for battle, and his features were so beautiful he seemed to glow. Not to be outdone, I too wore makeup in the field at first, but these days I do my best to look the rugged warrior type, throwing out my chest, tying my helmet low, and walking with a swagger.

We put Kusuné's presents in our makeshift storehouse and placed a sentry at the door. We were in a strong position, with a cliff at our backs and a cove in front—Kakutan even wanted to build our main fort there. A pine tree on the slope of a nearby hill, big enough for a goblin to sit in, would make an impromptu watchtower. It was just right for the job, since from its top one could take in the cove and the mainland, road and all, at a glance.

– Fukasu off to patrol the roads; the monk has ordered him to look out not for attacking Genji but for Heiké survivors escaping this way. By the ninth just past, Yoshitsuné had collected his troops and marched back to the capital, the palace being informed of his victory by special courier the day before. As we are in no danger from the Genji at the moment, Kakutan considers it more important to save the locals from the depredations of our own men along their escape route.

As we expected, Fukasu returned after nightfall with over thirty Heiké soldiers. They had formed a group and were about to evict some villagers from their houses, when they were restrained by Fukasu. Kakutan assembled all thirty under the oak, stood in front of the watch fire, and welcomed them with this little speech:

"Each of you has come a long way, through many hardships. I know you are all from the lord of Takiguchi's brave army in the hills above Ichinotani, but from today I would like you to think of yourselves as our comrades-in-arms. I have no doubt the lord of Takiguchi met a noble death, and you should do him credit. We can offer only a rough shelter with a straw curtain over it, but please try to make yourselves comfortable for the night."

. He then distributed some provisions that had been cooked in Kusuné's well water, and finally presented a sword to Fukasu for his good work.

– I am writing this behind my own "straw curtain." Kakutan is working on his Juei diary, as usual.

20th Day of the Second Month:
– Rain all day. It didn't prevent Kusuné from bringing over a score of packhorses laden with a contribution of lumber, as well as five carpenters to put it together. "I brought you some boards and pillars," he announced. Kakutan, abandoning yesterday's protocol, stood talking with him awhile under the oak.

– A chill confined me to my pallet, where I looked at a scroll of Suenari's called "Sketches of Camp Arrangements." Suenari had the men build a temporary roof over me to keep the rain from blowing in, then gave it to me to relieve my ennui. It shows a variety of plans for setting out a camp, classifying them generally into offensive and defensive, then into the Eight, the Fish-Scale, the Crane's-Wing, the Snake, the Crescent, the Half-Moon, the Arrow, the Square and Circle, the Flying Geese, the Dragon, the Cartwheel, etc., with explanations. Kakutan says the cordon of abatis he is laying out is what the scroll calls a Half-Moon formation and is supposed to be the best defense for a camp like ours. Miyaji Kotarō, whom we left at Ikuta Wood, used to favor the Fish-Scale and the Crane's-Wing—not surprisingly, as the book says they are commonly used for naval formations.

– After Kusuné had gone, Kakutan came and told me it was essential we raid Tomonotsu, where I had stayed before, as soon as possible. An ideal spot to attract cargo boats from all the other ports. A squadron of some two hundred of Yoshitsuné's cavalry was billeted there with guard boats, to exact a toll from each ship sailing the coastline off the Sanyō road. Those operating from Tomonotsu itself were exempt, but ships from all other ports in Bizen were being milked. Kusuné, himself of Bizen, had appealed to us to alleviate their distress. It was clear to my monk that Kusuné hoped to restore the prosperity of the ports in the area by destroying Tomonotsu. To that end, he would supply us with a fleet of thirty sail and provisions for all hands—our fighting strength in exchange for his wealth.

– Kakutan put the thirty stragglers under Fukasu and named Suenari leader of the whole expedition. This made a hundred altogether, divided among sixteen barges, one of which carried supplies. Pilots and cooks, together with the crews, were all locals recruited by Kusuné. As commander in chief, Suenari received the red banner of the Heiké from my hands. The occasion was a moving one for him, as his tears showed. We spread one of Kusuné's curtains under the oak as a temporary shrine, and performed the rites for his departure. Suenari wore white-shouldered armor over a robe with a diamond design on the hem, the cord of his five-sectioned horned helmet tightly tied. He carried his gold-accoutered sword, a powerful cane-bound bow he called "Shooting Star," and two dozen arrows with dyed feathers. With this same bow he had brought down the eagle from a pine tree on top of a cliff. His manner was relaxed, and his rugged physique and determined expression bespoke a splendid commander.

As the raiding party was leaving, a dozen horses arrived in camp as a further donation from Kusuné. Kakutan gave these to an equal number among the men left and bade them arm themselves; then, throwing his black-armored figure onto a cream-colored charger, he led them off sword-lance in hand to patrol the roads. This left only seven in camp, except for Gongorō of the Matsunaga party and his ten or so followers.

– Kusuné's five carpenters helped my people make a proper shelter, despite the rain. They began by erecting pillars with a ridgepole stretched between, and on this threw a plank roof; then laid the floorboards well off the ground. We had decided against commandeering farmhouses, in the hope of winning over the local people, since we intended to build a full-scale fort here in time. This policy seemed to bear fruit: by evening, a fellow from Samigahama called Shiaku no Bennai had arrived, to place himself unreservedly at my service. Gongorō told him, "Better go home and wait for orders." This Gongorō is a doughty provincial from Hashirijima, who revered my dead Miyaji as a model of samurai virtue.

I walked into the hut. The carpenters, addressing me through Gongorō, offered profuse apologies for its rough-and-ready quality. I in turn told Gongorō I was well pleased with such an elegant little dwelling. However, the sound of the rain on the board roof was so cold and melancholy I took out Kakutan's journal to cheer me up. In a pleasant, flowing script, reminiscent of Fujiwara calligraphy, the first part began:

> In defeat, we have still our mountains and rivers; even in a castle, spring comes, the trees put out green leaves and all the flowers their fragrance, announcing the cruel law that the mighty shall be infallibly cast down. . . .

He went on to describe our retreat to Fukuhara, with scenes of the burning of the Rokuhara, Komatsu, and Lord Kiyomori's estates, in full detail:

> Black smoke blotted out the sun, as though darkness had come at midday; of the Phoenix Palace only the bare foundations remain, and of the imperial carriage, a few wheel marks. . . .
>
> The fall of our clan is the outcome of an irresistible flow of events, and the present military regime is only the tyranny of Taira no Kiyomori taken one step further. The perfected form of this system of government will most probably be established by the firm hand of Minamoto no Yoshitsuné.

The writer had willy-nilly been swept up by the circumstances of the times, but hinted that he had thrown in his lot with us to follow the natural flow of things, and ultimately to escape the world.

I felt the sense of despair in what I'd read and rolled it up halfway through, returning it to the monk's armor chest.

– Later in the evening, he came back with half a dozen more stragglers. Men of Major General Arimori's, they had been part of the rout at Mikusa Hill, originally numbering ten or so, until caught by a group of three hundred armed peasants at Funasaka Pass and reduced to six.

– One of my men who'd been gone since yesterday, Seven-Leagues, turned up at nightfall. At a fishing village called Ushimado Landing, he fell in with some bonzes who had fled the capital, and heard the city's

96

recent news; he even brought a copy of a valuable document with him.

21st Day of the Second Month:
– Seven-Leagues' intelligence is that Ex-Emperor Goshirakawa put certain questions to his senior ministers on the ninth. While answering them, Minister of the Right Kanezané had tried to exonerate the clan as best he could. The Heiké, unlike Kiso Yoshinaka, were His Imperial Majesty's relatives, nobles, and vassals. Moreover, we still held the sacred regalia, and since it was of urgent importance to have them brought safely to the capital, it was folly—said he—to incur our resentment. In his opinion it was unreasonable to expose the heads of Heiké dead on Jail's Gate. The other ministers concurred.

Yoshitsuné was so enraged at this he went before the ex-emperor with tears in his eyes to refute it: "Is this why I faced death at Ichinotani," he said, "and fought to soothe the terrible bitterness of my father Yoshitomo's spirit? He proved his fidelity again and again in the Hōgen disorders, yet he was misunderstood and earned the imperial wrath. His head was paraded through the streets, his corpse hung up on Jail's Gate! The loyal retainer of yesterday was branded a traitor overnight. Even as a child, I sorrowed over my dead father's cruel fate. Now, in their turn, the Heiké, who once provided senior statesmen, are nothing but rebels. If I cannot see their heads displayed in the streets, from whence can I draw the strength to punish my emperor's enemies?"

The chief imperial adviser's face showed displeasure at this speech, but His Imperial Majesty had approved Yoshitsuné's declaration. On the thirteenth, the heads were assembled at Yoshitsuné's mansion in the Muromachi district and conveyed along Sixth Avenue to the riverbed. Poor Atsumori and others had their heads raised on lances with red pennants showing their names and, after being paraded through the streets, were exposed on Jail's Gate. There they were seen by many thousands of people, and it seems one of the pennants was mistakenly inscribed with my own name: Tomoakira. Indeed, Seven-Leagues insists that the bonzes mentioned me.

The document he managed to get a copy of was an imperial decree. The document was addressed to our chief councillor at Yashima by Lord

High Chamberlain Naritada, who was using the captive General Shigehira as a decoy:

> The previous emperor, Antoku, has now descended from the clouds of his northern palace into Kyūshū. The sacred regalia of jewel, sword, and mirror have been swallowed up in the mud of the southern islands; for many years they have preserved the imperial house, but may in time be a source of ruin for our country.
>
> His traitorous adviser, General Shigehira, who wantonly destroyed the Tōdaiji temple, was on the seventh of this month abandoned by his family on the beach at Ichinotani, there to be taken prisoner.
>
> The caged bird yearns for the clouds as it drifts a thousand leagues on the waves of the Southern Ocean; the returning wild geese call to their lost companion; will they be heard in the capital? Although the justice of such as Yoritomo demands that the death penalty should be exacted from Antoku's erring adviser, if the regalia are returned to the capital, even General Shigehira might be granted amnesty.
>
> By imperial decree, enacted in the third year of Juei, Second Month, from Lord High Chamberlain Naritada of the Imperial Household to the chief councillor of the Heiké.

Kakutan says that the form of this letter indicates a forgery made to circulate among the populace. However, we do know that an imperial decree of some kind was sent to Chief Councillor Tokitada on Yashima.

27th Day of the Second Month:
– With the help of Kusuné and Shiaku no Bennai, I assembled seventy laborers to begin work on the fort. Along with carpenters, there are smiths and bow-makers. Kakutan wants a strong enclosing wall and, among other things, a hall big enough to accommodate two hundred children; we are building a center of culture, it seems! His grandiose plan envisages something like a branch of the famous Kangaku Academy, where he would rise to the lectern himself to provide proper schooling for the children of the area. The sight of his big frame has already become

an indispensable source of pride to our camp. The workmen and carpenters are wonderfully braced up by him.

– Suenari has returned in triumph from Tomonotsu. The occupying force has been swept out of the town and its buildings reduced to ashes. Stayed there once on the way to our southern headquarters, and a girl from one of the cottages on the hill met me on the beach. I remember she did her hair in the Rokuhara fashion just for me. Suenari burned her house down with the rest, I suppose.

– They have proclaimed an almsgiving in the capital for funds to cast a new statue of the Buddha.

– Gongorō returned from Yashima today. A few days ago he ferried over to the imperial camp to find out the gist of the reply to the "decree." He reports the chief councillor to be in two minds about making peace with Yoshitsuné. The reply drafted by him can be summarized thus:

The continued absence of the imperial family and regalia from their proper place was in no way due to the reluctance of the Heiké to bring them back. As was well known, troops from the Kamakura region had been deliberately obstructing our return to the capital, so that postponement was only natural. Under the protection of spurious "decrees," the Genji regularly descended on us; we, on the other hand, were merely defending ourselves. We had not once engaged in battle without provocation. The Genji and Heiké had no real enmity between them. We knew how crucial it was to stop the war and bring to an end the present disastrous state of the world. We desired our twofold aim—that is, the return of the regalia and peace between the two clans—to be achieved by a full decree, conceived in justice to us. The ex-emperor's secretary had sent a letter to us at Ichinotani on the sixth, announcing the dispatch of an envoy on the eighth to ensure peace. Orders were supposedly sent to the Kamakura Genji not to take up arms again until the envoy's return to the capital. The Heiké in their turn had cautioned their soldiers to keep the truce at all costs. Despite this, on the seventh, the Kamakura troops in their customary "civilized" manner had attacked the imperial flagship. The Heiké, adhering to the "gracious decree," had not pressed the engagement; but the Genji, taking advantage of this, had escalated their attack into a regular battle, inflicting many casualties. Was this because the Genji were deliberately not notified of the truce? Or because they had ignored the decree? Or had the whole thing been a ruse to catch the Heiké off guard?

Such was the import of the answer, some five hundred and sixty characters long, sent to Lord High Chamberlain Naritada. As Kakutan had suspected, the "decree" of the sixth turned out to be a trick. The whole affair had been deplorable. To top it all off, General Shigehira was still under house arrest in the Toi mansion in Kyōto.

– Kakutan out with a party of ten to patrol the roads, but soon came back with three heads from Kamakura dispatch riders. One of the messengers carried a letter from Yoshitsuné himself, addressed to Kuninobu, a Tosa daimyō, to this effect: ". . . The Genji must rally all their loyal allies and, with their combined strength and determination, hunt the Heiké down."

The three couriers had intended to cross from Tomonotsu to Iyo, and ride on to Tosa by the land route.

1st Day of the Third Month:
– A man from Seno-o, in nearby Bitchū, rode into camp today and offered his sword. He is the son of Seno-o no Kaneyasu, who vanquished Kiso Yoshinaka's man Narizumi last October at the post station of Mitsuishi in his home province. However, in the battle at the fortress in Fukurinji-nawaté, Kiso's half brother Kanehira had done for him. Most of the family and retainers were killed as well. The son escaped danger by riding along the riverbank and lying low in godforsaken little villages like Ihara.

He is only a boy, hardly more than fourteen, but brings a band of a dozen horsemen with him; his green hunting outfit, held with a light green corselet, was his dead father's prized possession, and his mount, lead by an orderly, is a sturdy, well-fed animal. Despite his youth he looks promising.

As he knelt before me, I told him that the time to avenge his father would soon come, and my words of sympathy and encouragement greatly affected him. He was weeping with emotion as he retired from my presence. His retainers looked reliable enough, but their short-sleeved tunics tucked up at the back or persimmon-colored robes held with link corselets gave a shabby impression. Horses in good condition, though. – From today, will sleep at Kusuné's estate. My hut to be torn down and a proper fort built for us. With the coolies and carpenters at work, I shall only get in the way.

Stayed indoors all day. I thought to bring Kakutan with me, but he will be busy directing the affairs of the encampment. Promising to visit from time to time, he remained behind and in his place Suenari, or alternately Fukasu, is attending me. Koyata and Seven-Leagues are with me too.

Kusuné's place is quite comfortable. Its style is very grand even for the most powerful family of the region, and the apartments put at my disposal have a magnificent view. I can see pine woods, the sea, islands jutting up. . . . Koyata and Seven-Leagues are right next door and always join me when I take a turn around the garden. Fukasu on duty today; he is unequaled among all my troops, having the strength of ten and famous for the loudness of his voice. When standing to windward, he can be heard five hundred yards away. He's in the next room as I write, having his shoulders and arms rubbed by Seven-Leagues. At the moment, I am stretched out on a soft carpet by a bright, smokeless fire.

2nd Day of the Third Month:

– Over thirty retainers and about ten maids in the house. The men are usually engaged in unloading the ships newly arrived in the harbor, or loading the outgoing ones. The maids go barefoot when they're outside. Kusuné is twenty-three years old, his wife nineteen. His mother is all of forty, and a sister Chinu, who brings in my dinner tray, seventeen. A maid called Okozé brings in Seven-Leagues' and the others'.

After the sun went down a little while ago, Chinu showed by her manner that she was attracted to me—a gesture of courtesy to my men, as well as their commander. I suppose a general can hardly help being admired by beautiful young girls wherever he goes. I wanted to hint, with a restraint becoming my rank, that her interest was not unacceptable. When next she came near, with eyes demurely downcast, I put my hand on her shoulder. As luck would have it, Kakutan came on the scene at that very moment, being conducted around the garden by my host. He is leaving tomorrow morning to destroy the remaining forces of Minamoto no Yukiié. They are occupying a place called Kasaoka Landing in the next province of Bizen and, together with the pirate navies of Kōnoshima and Shiraishijima, are about to assault our flanks.

Yukiié was originally deputy governor of Bizen, Bitchū, and Harima, but was driven away by both Kiso Yoshinaka and the Heiké. He was last heard of at Takasago Bay, and where he's got to is anyone's guess. That was about the end of the Tenth Month last year, when the clan conquered Kiso's army at Mizushima.

Kakutan, knowing the importance of good communications in his "mopping up" operation, has already dispatched a fast boat to Yashima. This time he is leaving Suenari in charge of the camp and, minus the latter and his force, will have upwards of three hundred men with him. Of course, I am going too, as commander in chief.

Kakutan shut the door, leaving Chinu at a loss: should she continue our intimate scene, or leave it at that?

3rd Day of the Third Month:

– Our three hundred embarked in thirty boats, manned by experienced sailors and coolies recruited by Kusuné. By nightfall we had reached a place called Sotoura on Kōnoshima. Here we captured and interrogated a fisherman, who told us of a fort on the hill behind the village, held by over fifty men. Using the darkness as cover, we landed and took advantage of a sea wind to set fire to their stockade. Kakutan then led a group of our strongest, with Fukasu and Gongorō, into the fort and wiped out the defenders in a brief hand-to-hand battle. The monk swung his sword-lance to good effect, as usual, and Fukasu and Gongorō followed his example with their own weapons. It is the perfect tool for dealing quickly with a confused enemy. My arrows finished off those who tried to run away. By the time I had fitted the third to my bow, the battle was over.

Today's spoils are two hundred sacks of grain and three warships. Seno-o's men took the swords and armor of the dead.

We are staying in a fisherman's cottage. Dawn is just breaking.

4th Day of the Third Month:

– Occupied a place called Kitahama on Shiraishijima. Got a dozen boats and three hundred sacks of grain. Wounded in the right arm, and can't hold my brush. I am dictating this to Fukasu. In none of my engagements since the retreat from the capital have I known defeat, yet on this remote island, to be caught by vulgar bandits! My own fault. Kakutan brought off another of his fine maneuvers today.

The following addition, respectfully, by Fukasu no Kurō:
– Our noble lord sleeps quietly. His wound is not deep enough to worry us. He is only tired from loss of blood. Lord Kakutan is sitting composedly in one corner of the room, writing his "Juei Journal." We are in a fisherman's cottage in Kitahama on Shiraishijima. There is a great old matriarchal oak in the garden; of the many arrows that have skimmed past her trunk, only one has pierced the bark. It is evening, and the island across the bay is dyed a deep purple. . . .

Isle-on-the-Billows

Introduction

Of all the great religions of the world, Buddhism seems to be the easiest for a Christian (or, for that matter, an atheist) to admire. We think Islam fanatical, Hinduism idolatrous, Judaism encumbered with dietary laws. But Buddhism, ah! Buddhism is the religion of peace and contemplation, unconcerned with hierarchy or display, intent on personal enlightenment. And as even Billy Graham admitted once, its followers "are kind to animals."

Our attitude is partly due to the vogue for Zen, which in fact was heavily influenced by Taoism, and hardly represents the mainstream of orthodox Buddhism. Every human institution has its dark side: Buddhism in Tibet became a cult of death, and the stoic discipline of Zen and its martial arts were originally for combat as well as spiritual training. It is true that Buddhism has given rise to no religious wars in the sense of the Crusades, but as we see in "Waves," Japanese monasteries could produce thousands of soldiers, armed to the teeth, in support of their political intrigues. As for "kindness to animals," the next story shows how such idealism can, when taken to extremes, be as disruptive as the most cynical self-interest.

The great merit of Buddhism in Japan (as with Taoism in China) is that it provided a philosophical alternative to steadily hardening social discipline. Under the cult of loyalty (later dubbed *bushidō*) in the medieval period and the state Confucianism of the Tokugawa, samurai and commoner were expected to consider their social obligations first, last, and always. Buddhism, for all its emphasis on frugality and austerity, was an acceptable vehicle for mystical and artistic yearnings, as we may suppose it was for the shōgun Tsunayoshi when he decreed the Law of Compassion for Fellow Creatures. Not even he could force people to be "compassionate," but he could see that they were punished if they mistreated animals—which meant if they interfered with animals in any way.

Religion is of the heavens, human beings belong on earth, and the Japanese had made their peace with Buddhist-inspired vegetarianism long before this period. "Not eating animals" had become "not eating four-footed animals"—such as oxen, dogs, and horses, which were bred for other purposes anyway! Furthermore, raising large animals for food involved more expense than the average smallholder could afford. That left fish and fowl and "mountain whale" (as wild boar was euphemistically called). Ordinarily, as in Europe, wild boar and deer would be left for the aristocracy to hunt.

Which brings up a point that Ibuse makes in many subtle ways throughout "Isle": kindness to animals and aristocratic "love of nature" are a luxury for the poor. Animals represent wealth, and have to be caught, worked, and sold to the limit. The peasants' masters may preen themselves on their humanitarianism, because they can hire people to mistreat animals for them. And at the end of the story, nature rebels at the injustice. To put the point in a modern context: how many seal-hunters' wives can afford fur coats?

In his postscript to the 1970 revised edition of this story, Ibuse recalls that he finished it just one day before the first American jeep rolled into his native village of Kamo in Hiroshima Prefecture, where he was staying in his parents' house to wait out the raids and the famine in Tokyo. That he wrote the story at this particular juncture is quite significant: the long war had come to an end at last, but most Japanese cities were smoldering heaps of rubble, the exhausted population was at starvation point, and the shock waves of what happened in Hiroshima on the morning of August 6, 1945, were still being painfully felt throughout Ibuse's native prefecture. There were few villages in the larger Hiroshima area, even small, remote ones like his own, that didn't have someone in the city on that fateful day. Ibuse was not one of them, fortunately, but he had seen enough of the war—at very close range—as a war correspondent during the Fall of Singapore, where he was sent by the Imperial Army in 1941. He didn't like being inducted into the army, and what he saw it doing in Malaya he liked even less. Although many of his literary colleagues did, he never wrote patriotic articles praising the heroism of the Japanese soldier or supporting the official ideology of the Greater East Asia Co-prosperity Sphere. On the contrary, he came back a very angry man, critical not only of the military clique but of the whole ruling bureaucracy of established institutions—be it the army, the Buddhist clergy, or the political oligarchy.

This anger, at times almost an urge to see "official Japan" wiped off the face of the earth, found expression in several powerful stories written at this time. "Lieutenant Lookeast" (*Yōhai taichō*) is best known among them for its biting satire of the Imperial Army and its dehumanizing discipline. "Isle-on-the-Billows" (*Wabisuké*) is less of an obvious satire on the army and its tyranny over the common people, yet through its seemingly detached historical theme it presents a no less compelling caricature of the samurai bureaucracy. Ibuse's growing conviction that the common people's world had almost nothing to do with the one in which their superiors lived is symbolically expressed here by a more dramatic polarization than in the other story. There are many untranslatable intimations in the imagery of "Isle" that suggest this. Take the name of the island, Hadakajima: it is written with three characters meaning "High-Wave Island," but in its spoken form it conveys the double entendre of "Naked Island" (as the famous film was called), suggesting that this penal colony is a miniature version of Japanese society, with its complex power structure exposed in a more baldly obvious form. From the top of the social hierarchy where the well-meaning shōgun and his religious adviser issue a somewhat overzealous law, all the way down to the ambitious warden of a small penal colony, stretches a chain of imitation; by aping the mannerisms of their superiors, these social climbers hope to reach the same exalted status as their betters. In contrast to this ersatz world of bureaucrats, who can easily replace each other—note that the warden hasn't a single skill he can call his own— the common people (and especially their representative in the story, Wabisuké the Bird-Catcher) have each a craft that makes them individually unique. Anybody can become a warden and copy the refined way of beating prisoners by "drumming" on their backs, but nobody can catch four sparrows with one thrust of a fowling rod, or tell at a glance what kind of bird is nesting high in the branches of a tree, as Wabisuké can.

Although the author does not idealize him in any way—he is an earthy working man, inarticulate and socially clumsy at times—his name combines a wealth of connotations that suggest he is more than simply "everyman." Wabisuké not only translates as "companion in solitude," it is the name of a small, modest, yet elegant variety of camellia.

A contemporary Western reader who has had no experience of life in an authoritarian society may find some passages a little hard to take: for example, why do Uetoku the gardener and his friend the estate guard not vent their anger more openly when one of them gets flogged by the steward? They are obviously out of earshot in the guard's hut and yet they talk about the caning as if admiring some display of skill. We find here one of Ibuse's favorite stylistic techniques: what might be called "oblique criticism through irony"; but it is also a realistic portrayal of the Japanese reluctance to criticize one's superiors too bluntly and openly. There is always a chance that of the two people needed for a discussion, one will turn informer, or someone else will overhear them—little wonder in a close-packed country with no solid walls in a Western sense. This being the case, words of mock admiration for the master's skill at punishment provide a safe expedient: the peasants are supposed to be inherently stupid and incapable of irony; to officially admit that their communication has more subtle levels than its face value would be intolerable for the official class. A careful exchange of sarcasm allows the two men to feel each other out, and when they realize they have both tasted the rod, they become more openly critical of their superiors. The Afro-American novelist, Richard Wright, in his autobiography *Black Boy*, describes a very similar need for circumspection in the southern states, where not so very long ago a black man who spoke with an educated accent was suspected of "sass" and liable to violent punishment.

Throughout the story Ibuse not only parodies the hypocrisy of samurai officials and Buddhist bonzes (to whom the well-meant Law of Compassion comes to serve as a vehicle for personal advantage and a tool for pestering the common people) but questions the very essence of aesthetic tradition. He seems to be saying that the aristocratic cult of nature, with its moon-viewing parties and picnics under blossoming cherry trees where genteel poems are exchanged, belongs to a narrow, privileged world to which peasants and artisans have no access. When Warden Onohachi sends an amorous haiku to Osugi, neither she nor the crafty Tōkichi know what to do with it. Tōkichi dismisses it as a joke: "Can you see me making a haiku?" Osugi is a real farm girl of flesh and blood, not the stereotyped "country lass" of poetic convention, and, like Wabisuké, has to cope with natural forces more tangible than the elegant images of court poetry. Yet if they don't appreciate such idealized lyrical images, it doesn't mean that these people are less sensitive to "nature" than their superiors. It's just that their perceptions are less filtered through the *haute culture* of established poetry and that they put more trust in what their senses tell them; after all, they make a living not by reading poems, but reading the "language" of nature directly by smell, touch, and sound. What Wabisuké lacks in verbal culture, he makes up in manual skills: it is difficult to imagine nowadays, when the old craft of bird-catching is practically extinct, that someone could have caught four sparrows at one thrust of a lime-stick. He doesn't lack real poetic sensitivity either—we note that when he climbs the gnarled old pine tree on the mountain, he lingers a few moments to take in "the moan of the wind through the pine needles." Another favorite image of classical poetry, but how many court poetasters would have gone to the source?

The portrayal of Wabisuké's female companions is realistic enough, especially that of the big fishing girl Omon; yet comparing the two women we may wonder what the author's purpose is in bringing together such contrasting types. Omon couldn't be more down-to-earth, but let us look more closely at Osugi. As always in Ibuse, Osugi's tragic story is presented with humorous overtones. We learn that her convulsive crying fit was brought on by seeing traces of a recent forest fire and that she has good reason to fear such a fire. What made her "crime" really grave is not the fact that her so-called negligence caused considerable damage to her fellow farmers' property, but rather that a family of badgers died on her mountain, and went unreported into the bargain. This is the ironic, conscious surface of the text, but underneath we can hear the deeper symbolic connections suggested by Ibuse's unique turn of phrase: Osugi's weeping fit is described as having a "glowing charm," and an "almost smoldering quality." Such terms are unusual, yet the image brings together the two elements of fire and water, echoing the real fire and flood that shaped Osugi's life; the eruption of Osugi's "blood storm" and her tears reenact the fire and the flood from the broken dam in her home district. This flood of tears washes away all her fear and frustration and, far from irritating Wabisuké, calms him and purges his own anger and fear—the "grime" of his soul—in a sort of symbolic purification.

While the language of the officials is of a stilted, at times bombastic kind, the common people speak a rich colloquial Japanese, and the passages describing their daily activities abound in dynamic, colorful verbs. Once in a while Ibuse will use a striking metaphor, such as "Osugi was still wailing into the earth, as if trying to break it open," or "(the song) came out like a sutra chanted at the bottom of a river." Again, we see that while the samurai bureaucracy moves about in a shallow, puppet-like world, the people are in touch—not through words, but through their very existence—with the elemental forces of the Japanese soil. Osugi wails into the ground on the mountain where they work, and deep in the entrails of another mountain, this time the great Fuji itself, a larger "blood storm" is gathering.

When the underground anger erupts toward the end, it takes away the whole "living Hell" of the island, along with the warden and his henchmen. And when the angry waters of the Fuji River swallow the Isle, washing away what the Japanese of those days would have called its *kegare* (ritual impurity), we witness another purification rite, this time on a cosmic scale. We note that "all that could be seen were high waves washing the river's banks" just where the sinister Mole of Hell juts out above the water. Every time Wabisuké climbs the mountain, he long-ingly watches the distant figure of an official or a boatman fishing for trout from this cliff. He wouldn't mind fishing himself, and the ban on prisoners fishing has intensified the pain of his exile. In a hard-working, feudal country there were no sports in the modern sense, and fishing was the people's only accepted form of "recreation."

Hours before the island sinks into the river, Wabisuké once again watches this hateful place from the top of the mountain, shading his eyes against the sunlight. Suddenly he realizes that his posture is that of prisoners who have been released from the Isle and are returning home. But he also looks like Urashima Tarō, the legendary young fisherman who spent a pleasant year in the Dragon King's palace at the bottom of the ocean with the beautiful naiad Otohimé. Now there is no reason why Wabisuké should hope to return home at this particular moment. His eyes are not looking at the princess Otohimé, but at the hateful island. Yet his mind's eye, perhaps sensing what's coming, looks into the Dragon King's palace and urges the ruler of the underwater kingdom: come fast and take this horrible place away. And when the waters do just that, we can sense both the power of the water deities and their generosity in the description of the Isle's destruction. In this context, the fact that the girl Omon, prosaic as she may be, comes from "Dragon King's Village" is not a mere coincidence, for she is also in touch with the depths, not least through her trained cormorants that dive in the river for fish.

So what we witness in the dramatic finale of the story is really a tableau of "sinking Japan" or, rather, "official Japan" being wiped off the map. Why else would Ibuse close his story with Wabisuké's eyes holding the deeply imprinted image of red poppies against the snow-white waterspout that swallowed the Isle? There is no mistaking the familiar colors of the sun-disk flag of Japan.

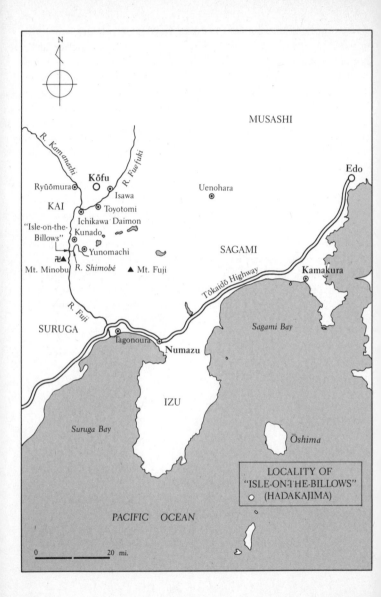

N

MUSASHI

Edo

R. *Kamanashi*

R. *Fuefuki*

Kōfu

Ryūōmura

Isawa

Uenohara

KAI

Toyotomi

Ichikawa Daimon

"Isle-on-the-Billows"

Kunado

卍▲

SAGAMI

Yunomachi

Mt. Minobu

R. *Shimobé*

▲ Mt. Fuji

Kamakura

Tōkaidō Highway

R. *Fuji*

SURUGA

Tagonoura

Sagami Bay

Numazu

IZU

Suruga Bay

Ōshima

PACIFIC OCEAN

LOCALITY OF
"ISLE-ON-THE-BILLOWS"
○ (HADAKAJIMA)

0 ————— 20 mi.

Isle-on-the-Billows

Along the Fuji River there are seven villages famous for their eel fishing. One of them is Hadakajima in the province of Kai—or more correctly, Hadaka Village of West Yatsushiro County in modern Yamanashi Prefecture. It stands just where the Shimobé River meets the Fuji, and where a few farmhouses, set among hillside vegetable gardens and the odd paddy field, skirt the edge of a mountain. This is a couple of miles downstream from the mouth of the valley in which the Shimobé's hot springs lie. The Fuji River spreads its banks far apart here, but before the Hōei period (A.D. 1704–11) it was wider still, enough for silt to form a solid mass in midstream. Trees grew there, allowing the odd cottager to work his rice paddy or kitchen garden behind a windbreak of pines. It was this big sandbank they called Hadakajima, or "Isle-on-the-Billows." One day early in the Sixth Month of the lunar calendar, three years before Mt. Fuji's greatest eruption in the fourth year of Hōei, there was a violent earthquake, and Hadakajima vanished overnight, houses and all.

Three years before that, the local magistracy had taken over the island and made it a penal farm for those under sentence of banishment—mainly for violation of the Law of Compassion for Fellow Creatures that so harassed the people of that time. The number of those punished under this law from the province of Kai alone never fell below a hundred a year; about thirty of these would be banished and, packed like sardines in a court jailhouse, they would wait for a ferry to penal islands far at sea: Hachijōjima, Miyakejima, or Niijima. But during this period, there was such a flood of exiles from the Edo area there was no room on these three for exiles from other parts of the country. So Hadakajima was made an auxiliary to the "main" islands, though it doesn't seem to have been the same kind of place as those grim, storm-bound coasts.

As criminals go, the inmates were small fry compared to the hard cases of Miyaké and Hachijō. Even so, the verdict was given in the same familiar words, and prisoners were all "banished to remote Isle-on-the-Billows." A warden was assigned to the colony through proper channels, and convicts disobeying his orders were given the lash. Those who slacked at their work were given suitable punishment—in that way it was no different from other islands. A particularly unruly prisoner might be hanged, and a special beech tree was brought all the way from Suruga Province for the purpose and planted near the ferry dock. This detail, too, was to be found on Hachijō and Miyaké. Only, instead of needing a boat to escape, convicts could wait till the river went down and wade across to shore; but for all that it was still called "the grave crime of boat escape."

The other difference on this island was that the chief guard, who reported directly to the warden, had a staff of twelve men under him. Prisoners doing hard labor were ferried over to "the outside world" in separate details, each supervised by a guard.

The third in "line of succession" of Hadaka's wardens was a samurai named Ono Hachirōemon, known to his charges as "Onohachi." He had been selected from among subordinates of the warden of Miyakejima. This fellow had modeled himself on his former superior in every detail—in the way he fixed his topknot, the way he walked, even the way he spoke. Nearly forty, with an egg-shaped skull and downward-slanting eyes, he was no beauty, but always took the greatest pains with his toilette. When he gave orders to the convicts, he would pump his arm up and down to put more authority into his voice. His swagger would change, too, in time with his gestures. Picking up a handy stick to spank one of his charges, he wouldn't wave it wildly, like a ruffian with a bamboo sword, but as if he were beating out the time on a laced drum. Then he would stop the punishment and, trying not to break his smooth rhythm, throw the stick away and tap his fingertips lightly together, as though brushing off dirt. His hair fitted close to his head, topknot twisted slightly to one side for an extra touch of chic.

Now, there was on this island a bird-catcher named Wabisuké who had once been sent to Miyakejima, pardoned, then shipped off again to Hadaka. This man, as one of Miyaké's "old lags," had seen Onohachi's face before. He was familiar with that habit of swinging the arms and drumming on prisoners' backs with a stick. How could he have forgotten the dainty little twist of that topknot! He also knew from whom such mannerisms were copied: the warden of his former prison. He knew, moreover, that even this worthy was not the original—that Miyaké's warden had them from a high-ranking retainer in the Ido house (one Mondayū) who in his turn imitated Yanagisawa Yoshiyasu.

Lord Yanagisawa of Mino was an up-and-coming minister connected with the shōgun's house; as Uetoku, his fellow exile on Miyaké, had told Wabisuké: "At times like that, old Mondayū'd scowl at you fierce and dignified, like a lion. But underneath it he was cool, cool as a cucumber. . . . Still, the two're as different as night and day—Lord Yanagisawa's a hundred times fiercer, and colder too, than Master Mondayū!"

This Uetoku had been a gardener with the privilege of regular admission to the grounds of the Ido estate in Edo. Once he'd been there to do some trimming and discovered several night herons' nests in an ornamental pine, with hungry little birds in them. Bringing the nests gingerly down, he had set them on a rock. But after he went back up the tree to finish his work, the master's dog came along and made a terrible mess of the nests. It had killed three of the little birds in no time and eaten two or three others, when the dreaded Law of Compassion for Fellow Creatures flashed into Uetoku's mind. To protect the remaining chicks, he brandished his shears to chase the dog away, but the beast turned on him and pounced at the nest clutched in Uetoku's arms. It backed away when his blade grazed its shoulders, only to return to the attack, growling fiercely. Uetoku tried to climb the tree with one hand and protect the nest with the other, but it slipped out and fell into the pond. The dog remained clamped to his foot. He tried to shake it off, inching his way up the tree, and calling for help as loudly as he could. Drawn by the uproar, an estate guard and one of the pages, then a steward, came running to pull the dog off and quiet him. After shinnying back down, Uetoku retrieved the nest from the pond, but the chicks had been soaked with water and drowned. The page boy examined them and turned to the steward: "Alas, the little creatures have breathed their last."

The steward spoke sternly to Uetoku. "You must have been mad. Wait here and don't move." He passed the tiny corpses for the page to carry before they marched off together. After a moment, the boy returned to lead Uetoku out of the garden to the veranda of the stewards' apartments.

Three stewards with sour faces made their appearance. The matter had become serious. After a while, their superior, Head Steward Mondayū, came out in full regalia to announce in a voice quiet enough to give Uetoku the shivers, "It seems you have gravely injured the dog. Moreover you are responsible for the deaths of young herons nesting in the garden of our house." Uetoku scraped his forehead in kowtows, as though trying to bury himself, but the head steward went on, relentless, waving his arms and frowning fiercely.

"You stupid wretch! You have sullied the honor of our house. Look at me! Higher authorities will make their judgment known when it pleases them; time will tell what it is. But here we shall deal with you in our own way."

Stepping down into his clogs, he strode up to Uetoku and took hold of a broken bow leaning against the low fence around a peony bed. He raised it in an affected pose, like the drummer of a classical *hayashi* orchestra. But instead of a drum, he bore down on Uetoku's shoulders.

"Trembling like a leaf, eh, you scoundrel!" He applied a half-dozen stylish strokes and set the bow back up against the fence. Then he lightly tapped his open hands together, finger to finger, to flick off some invisible dirt. These mannered gestures did nothing to help Uetoku, and before getting to the ritual "Thank you for punishing me," he fainted dead away.

He woke up to find the familiar face of the watchman by his pillow. His friend had brought him to a dim-lit hut where the man ate and slept and now sat waiting.

"Was I out long?" he asked, but the watchman told him, "Doesn't seem so. You came to quicker than most."

On this estate, the flogging of servants was obviously not uncommon, and Uetoku, quite in tune with his own estimate of the situation, said in mock surprise, "His honor's putting a lot of style into the punishment these days, isn't he?"

The watchman was less impressed. "Style nothing! Yanagisawa the

Lord of Mino's style is the thing to see. Yanagisawa's quiet—no shouting—but fierce and dignified. You wouldn't dare cross him." And he added, "All the samurai with their sights on advancement try to cut the same figure. Why, even actors do it onstage: plastering their hair down tight to their skulls and waving their arms when they give orders. It's Lord Yanagisawa they're all copying, and they pass it on from one to another." This watchman too had once tasted the rod and the memory rankled, so he cheerfully went on finding fault with his betters.

On Miyakejima, Uetoku had passed on this "inside story" to Wabisuké. He knew it wasn't idle servants' gossip. In earlier days on Miyaké, Onohachi had roared at the top of his voice and, grabbing a stick or a length of bamboo, swung it over his head like a sword and thrashed his victims with a will. But the moment he was raised to warden of Isle-on-the-Billows, he became conscious of his performance, and a touch of class crept into his manner.

Plain folk have a gift for intuition. As the old adage says: "The people are like a mirror." Without Wabisuké joining in any malicious gossip, the other convicts on the Isle had got the whole story about Ono's affected manners. Adding a little flavor to the tale they would say, "Onohachi got beatings like that when he was Lord Yanagisawa's sandal-bearer . . . and prayed to Buddha every morning for a promotion, so he could do it to others!" The ferryman had whispered this story to the chief guard, and from him it reached the ear of Onohachi himself. The warden wasn't one to let something like that go by.

A glance at the prisoners' files told him that of the 105 convicts on Hadaka, the only one with "banishment to Miyaké" on his record was Wabisuké. "Onohachi's got something up his sleeve," Wabisuké thought, foreseeing a cruel revenge.

Onohachi's plot began as expected. When the chief guard lined up the prisoners for their orders next morning, he called Wabisuké out and told him to step closer.

"You're being made head trusty," he said. "I hope you know how lucky you are." Then he addressed the whole assembly.

"Now listen, men! It has pleased Master Ono to make Wabisuké the Bird-Catcher head trusty from today. Tōkichi the Gambler, who's been trusty till now, has been taken off. I want those two, and the rest of you, to remember that."

Wabisuké was a new arrival on the island. His promotion was obviously not a favor given to make his stay happier, or for any such weak-minded purpose. There was a stir in the ranks until Tōkichi the Gambler raised his gong-like voice.

"Shut up, all of you! . . . Well, Bird-Catcher, what do you say? Let's change the guard."

At the word of command, all were silent. Tōkichi must have guessed what Onohachi had in mind. He called out again, in the same ringing tones, "All together now. The iron hand!"

The convicts, Wabisuké with them, started clapping their hands in unison, with a shan! shan! shan! sound. The camp's response nearly ruined Onohachi's mean-minded plan: to have the new man's unfair promotion to first on the roll call provoke the inmates' resentment.

They prepared to leave on their work details. Wabisuké collected his fowling rod and bird whistle and went to call at the Gambler's hut:

"Thanks for the honest way you've treated me," he said formally. "I'm grateful. When we get a chance, let's pretend we're back in the outside world for one night, and I'll pledge your health in hot saké. Meantime, I'd be honored by any advice you could give me."

The Gambler, who was winding around his arm the hempen cord he would need at work, paused with a bitter smile. "Don't give me a pain. What advice can I give you? Wait a little—the wind'll change again."

Sure enough, the conch shell blew an unscheduled signal for assembly. Caught in the middle of preparations, convicts dashed to the parade ground, some with tools in their hands, others empty-handed. By ones and twos, carrying hoes and axes and saws, straw litters, mattocks and matchets and bamboo ladders, they came running up. The Gambler had a coil of palm rope, and Wabisuké a bamboo tube at his belt, a pack on his back, and a fowling rod in his hand. Under the pine tree on the parade ground stood Warden Onohachi, dressed up in a kind of fancy court out-fit, with the chief guard and a dozen men behind him. As the new head trusty, Wabisuké reported all present and accounted for, in a halting voice. At that point, three women prisoners showed up, running along a raised path between some poppy fields. One carried a large wooden birdcage, and the two others struggled with a bamboo litter for carrying earth. Their awkward burdens made them slap their feet down noisily as they ran. This seemed to irritate the warden, for he roared out, "What's that racket?" Shifting his grip on the whip he was holding, he shouted at Wabisuké, "Head trusty! Didn't you report all present?" and flew into a rage. "You blockhead! You're too incompetent to be a trusty. I'm returning your post to the former man. Do you hear me?"

Wabisuké tried to speak with authority. "Tōkichi the Gambler, step forward." Hiding the tremor in his voice, he shouted, "All together . . . the iron hand!" And as before, they all clapped their hands in unison.

Onohachi shifted the whip again and said in an ominous tone, "You women come here."

The three culprits crept forward and flung themselves down before the warden. One of them said, "A guard told us to wait by the ferry dock." Not satisfied with this, Onohachi lifted his chin at the chief guard, who stepped forward to wave the rest of the convicts back to work. They quickly disappeared—afraid to cough, let alone talk. They knew how often the lash fell on bystanders, too.

Wabisuké was behind the Gambler as they walked to the dock. The man gave a guffaw. "Listen, can you make a haiku?" he said and, when Wabisuké had answered "You joking?" confided, "Well, did you see that little looker carrying the birdcage on her back? She wants a poem to answer her beau. 'Make me a haiku,' she says, 'to go with this verse: To a country lass something-or-other in spring . . .'" The Gambler snorted. "Can you see me making a haiku? Anyway, looks like she didn't think of one, 'cause she's getting the works for it right now!" Wabisuké had a good idea who the "beau" might be, but knew better than to spell it out.

Several people had reached the dock before them and were stretched out on the beach. Other little groups came walking after Wabisuké and Tōkichi. Tied to the mooring post were two other boats besides the warden's, which was a lavishly painted affair in red lacquer covered by a thatched awning. Its boatman had scrambled onto a shiny black boulder jutting out in the water called the "Mole of Hell" and was fly-fishing for trout. The other two ferrymen had stopped fishing, and were just maneuvering their craft closer to the jetty when the guards arrived.

The prisoners lined up, and the chief guard called the roll from his ledger. The men had been notified the day before of what was to be done, but here on the beach they were divided into work details with specific directions. One gang was going to the newly cultivated land on the hills across the river. Five guards and the head trusty would oversee them. A second gang, led by one guard only, would build rafts where the rivers met nearby. The third team under another guard would collect cast-off straw sandals and horse manure along the roads, and a fourth was sent off to catch birds. When the chief guard called out the names of the fourth gang, a ripple of surprise swept the ranks of prisoners.

"Wabisuké the Bird-Catcher!" he called, and next, "Osugi from Kunado!" He closed the ledger with a final, "Carry on."

Now, Osugi from Kunado was the very woman who had just been punished by the warden. Her dimpled face was not at all bad-looking, her full figure surprisingly graceful.

No guard was assigned to them.

The two ferryboats made the trip to the opposite shore and back many times before Wabisuké and Osugi got in. He noticed a burning welt below the girl's right earlobe, where Onohachi's whip had bitten into her flesh. Getting out on the other side, they could hear the sound of trees being cut down on the hillside as men cleared the land for new fields. The two had started along the road below when they saw Tōkichi and one of the guards up in the woods.

"Hey, Bird-Catcher!" the Gambler hailed him, "don't forget your bird-call." He came running after them, making motions of handing something over. When he had caught up, he pressed two large coins into Wabisuké's palm and lowered his voice.

"Look sharp . . . they're waiting for you two to go over the hill. Take this—you'll need it on the road," he whispered, "but remember, if you get caught, it means your necks . . . so watch your step—you're playing with fire!" After blurting this out, he rushed back up the road. Under the guard's watchful eye, Wabisuké could neither ask for an explanation nor return the "travel money." The Gambler ran to the guard and bobbed his head respectfully, all innocence.

Wabisuké strolled off the high road and followed a mountain path, mimicking a crow's call with his bird whistle. Osugi trudged along after him with the cage slung on her back. As he felt much too bashful to speak, he was silent. Osugi had nothing to say either. The path soon faded out, and they climbed up the hillside along the bank of a stream until they had reached a wide clearing left by a forest fire. Here and there in the expanse of scorched soil, bracken already showed its green tips. Away below, through shimmering summer haze, they caught a glimpse of the Isle and some people fishing aboard the red lacquered barge. Still blowing his birdcall, Wabisuké crossed the parched ground until he spied a crow's nest in a pine hanging off a cliff and saw his chance to capture the parent birds. He had brought some rice straw; he would have to weave it together before smearing it thickly with birdlime, and arrange it carefully around the nest. But first he had to climb high up the tree with a bamboo tube of birdlime and water dangling at his hip and a handful of straw hanging from his sash like a tail. He handed the fowling rod to Osugi, and lightened his load to one sheaf of straw and the birdlime case. He then tied a pale yellow towel around his face, and relieved himself nearby. His preparations were complete.

The pine tree leaned slightly out from the cliff face, but luckily its trunk was rough; he needed no special skill to climb a tree like this. He scrambled up, making sure the adult birds were not at home. Quickly he set his trap, smearing lime on the straw and spreading it around the nest. The nestlings' eyes were already open, their black feathers sprouting. At the light touch of Wabisuké's hand on their heads, they stretched out their little necks and squeaked with hunger. But it wasn't the chicks he was after, so after catching a pleasant whiff of their raw, slightly sour smell, he slid off the tree to make his way back down the cliff. The ground there was thick with vegetation: ferns sprang up everywhere and fallen tree trunks had grown furry coats of green moss. There was one tree, a maple of surprising girth, that cast ample shade with its leaves. Hiding behind its trunk, Wabisuké peered up through the leaves at the cliff, catching glimpses of the pine branch that held the nest. There he was quickly joined by Osugi, still carrying the cage and holding the pole. When she sat down next to Wabisuké, the fragrance of her damp skin close by was delightful. He was annoyed with himself, for his body began to tremble and wouldn't stop. He could hear his heart pounding.

123

Wild thoughts of offering her the coins Tōkichi had given him rose in his mind; then he recalled the Gambler warning him to "watch his step," and calmed himself.

Wabisuké kept staring up at the cliff, but the old birds didn't show up. He noticed Osugi's shoulders were still heaving. How well it suited her, trying to sit as still as possible. It helped to control his own excitement.

"To a country lass something-or-other in spring . . . ," he said without thinking. "You asked the Gambler for a haiku, didn't you? What was it for?"

Osugi giggled. "The warden wanted to exchange poems, that's all. It was during the fuss over the baby they found on the west bank of the river. When I asked him, Master Tōkichi only said 'A haiku? From me?' . . . Oh, it's such a nuisance, really." She sighed a little affectedly, like a woman of the world.

Wabisuké didn't take this too seriously. " 'The country lass' and so on sounds like a love poem to me," he suggested. "If that's what he wants, why not play along and answer him back the same way?" But he really knew nothing of haiku etiquette, and his heart shrank at the thought that Osugi might ask *him* to compose her reply.

Then he saw one of the parent crows flying toward them from the hillside. It floated high over the clifftop and back, calling out several times, a question in its voice. Wabisuké put the birdcall to his mouth, and a cry of shrill answer came from above the cliff. Then nearer, from the pine tree, he heard the wingbeat break as the snared bird went into a spin and plummeted into a thicket, brushing the leaves of their maple on its way. Wabisuké dashed out and seized the bird. Osugi turned up a little flap over a window in the cage, which was completely covered in black cloth, and waited. There were crosspieces dividing the cage lengthways and sideways into a number of smaller compartments. Each had a little window with a flap of black cloth to close it. Wabisuké used a bran bag to remove sticky straw from the crow's feet and wings. He had joined several plaits of straw to make a length of five or six feet; the bird had got some tangled around its feet, and coiled around its body and wings. After carefully picking the straw off—he didn't want a bald bird on his hands—he shut the crow up in the cage. Its mate was cawing angrily around the clifftop. Soon this bird too got stuck to the remaining straw by the nest and came tumbling down with a broken flutter of one free wing. Grazing the cliff face, it did a fast loop and landed in the soft underbrush. Wabisuké was able to grab hold of it with no trouble.

The next thing was to get the nestlings down from the pine branch. Earning his living by scrounging in kite or crow nests held no interest for Wabisuké. Back in "the outside world," he had never taken a common crow or a kite. The Law of Compassion for Fellow Creatures had ruined his regular trade, but he still got under-the-counter orders from the wealthy dealers of Kōfu who wanted somewhat rarer species. For birds to be pickled in salt and delivered to Edo and Ōsaka, to the great houses of the realm or the priests of Mt. Minobu, he had hunted and made his deliveries in the utmost secrecy. After serving an apprenticeship from the age of eight, and some twenty more years in a ruthless business, his reputation among clients was well earned. He took special orders only: for mountain pheasant, duck and mandarin duck, quail, winter sparrow, and thrush. Now and then someone wanted live quail or wild goose. Once, with an order for live geese, he was asked to gather kaya nuts, chestnuts, mushrooms, and citrons from the same mountain region he would take the birds. Puzzled by the request, he had inquired about the connection and been told that the bigwigs placing the order were convinced the delicate flavor of fowl could only be brought out by fruit and vegetables from the same locale. Investigating a little further, he found that a high official from Edo was paying a quiet visit to a local estate, and the geese were to be the special course at a gala dinner accompanying the tea ceremony. Money was squandered almost sinfully on these parties, and Wabisuké risked prison or banishment each time, to provide the food. Never mind: he was a bachelor and liked being his own man. And the hunting—even the killing—of his "fellow creatures" gave him a deep, inexplicable thrill.

It was still early in the season when they caught him goose-hunting and sent him to Miyakejima for three years' hard; soon after being paroled he was caught again. It had happened on the way to a millionaire's villa, to deliver live ducks; he was about to smuggle them through the service gate when a gang of urchins loitering nearby heard one of them quack and gave him away. So certain was he their bills were tied with tatami cord and wrapped in cloth, the first "quack!" made his heart stop. That he didn't get a long-standing patron in trouble was a matter of sheer luck; and he would need some more if he ever hoped to get away from Isle-on-the-Billows. "I wonder," he thought, "if I should just smash these nestlings against a rock and run away?" Then he thought a little further: "Would Osugi go with me?"

"No good," he decided, "we'd lose our heads if we were caught. I'd be playing right into bloody old Onohachi's hands. Plain foolish."

After he was done with the crow chicks, Wabisuké washed his hands and face in a pond almost buried by the underbrush; the water was cold, but since Osugi was looking on, he stripped and jumped in to show off a little. But when he looked up, Osugi was gone.

"Oy!" he shouted, and "Hoy!" the answer came back from the top of the cliff. He went up and found her plumped down in the shade of a tree, a little apart from where they'd left the cage. Refreshed after his swim, Wabisuké greeted her cheerfully. "Enough work. Let's eat."

Lunch for the two of them was a hamper full of boiled millet from the island's soup kitchen. When you dug down into it with your chopsticks, you'd find a small lump of *miso*. This was to be divided in two for their afternoon tea. Before taking up her chopsticks, Osugi sat upright on the grass with eyes shut and hands joined, as prescribed before meals on Hadaka. You were expected to give thanks from the bottom of your heart to both gods and officials for the daily bread which, in their infinite mercy, they had provided. You also swore to work hard and take regulations to heart. These rules meant little to Wabisuké. Instead of praying, he waved his chopsticks through the air as if chasing a gnat; tracing its "flight," he touched his food almost as if by accident, then dug right in. He could still smell Osugi's skin, but his heart was calm now and his body at ease. He joined in her lighthearted banter, nodding to her in an easygoing way. Osugi was saying that the sight of the charred hillside where fire had raged put a knot in her stomach. For all that, she ate her millet with apparent relish. Pointing her chopsticks at the cage, she asked him: "Those crows—grown-up ones can't be fed by hand, can they?"

Wabisuké shook his head. "Don't worry. When we take them back to the island, a courier will rush them to the magistrate's office. Two special attendants'll be waiting for them in his aviary. They get an allowance of ten sacks of rice each—'course they don't have my know-how. . . ."

Osugi's eyes widened. "Ten sacks each? My heavens!"

"Are you surprised?" said Wabisuké. "Up in Edo, the shōgun has four commissioners just to look after his kennels. His honor's no skinflint: each one gets three hundred sacks of rice in salary, I've heard, and a dozen grooms to help 'em. Why, they make our warden look small! Those pampered mutts get five fingers of white rice a day, half a pint of sardines, and all the *miso* they can eat. They rank way above us, you know." He laughed, pleased by his own eloquence.

But tears had welled into Osugi's eyes. "You just made that up," she gasped. "It's some bogey tale to frighten kids—not about the shōgun." She shut her mouth tight.

"No, no," Wabisuké insisted, "it's no tale. One of my mates told me when I was on Miyaké. He knew all about it—worked under a kennel boss. In one day, the palace dogs'd gulp down two tons of rice. In a single day!"

Without warning, a howl burst from Osugi's throat and floods of tears poured down her cheeks. Taken aback, Wabisuké turned apologetic.

"Hold on, now . . . sorry. I'm sorry!"

Osugi's crying grew violent, she covered her face and rocked back and forth in anguish; she fell forward and wailed into the ground. Wabisuké was frantic. What if the guards heard? Or if a woodcutter happened by, he'd think the worst.

Growing more and more confused, Wabisuké said, "Don't do that, don't. It's no good crying out here in the mountains. What did I do? Stop!" and patted her on the back. Then, afraid it might be misunderstood, he snatched back his hand and looked around him.

Not a soul was in sight. Osugi was still wailing into the earth, as if trying to break it open. Wabisuké tiptoed around her and pleaded: "I won't say a word more! About the shōgun or anything . . . come on, don't cry. I'm sorry I said anything." But Osugi waved away his apologies and blurted out between wails:

"I want to hear it—all of it!"

"What?" Wabisuké was baffled. "You don't mean that."

The crying stopped. "Tell me." Swallowing her sobs, Osugi sounded almost passionate. "Tell me the whole story, please. About the Dog Shō-gun and all, to the last detail—don't spare me!"

Wabisuké looked around again and saw no one there. Osugi went on bawling for some time. When she finally stopped, she got the hiccups. They were like little convulsions, rising from mysterious depths. With her hands wrapped around her face, she might have been waiting, quivering, for a hammer's blow. Ah, he thought, must be what people in the country called a woman's "blood storm." He began very tentatively, as if touching a sore spot: "I . . . I reckon I can tell you what I know, anyway. About the shōgun's dogs, eh, and the fat life they lead? Is that what you want?"

Osugi, still hiccuping, nodded her head earnestly.

"Where'll I start? I heard the story from Gorōmatsu on Miyaké. . . ." Wabisuké racked his brains for details and decided she would most want to hear about the magnificence of the kennels.

According to Gorōmatsu, a sumptuous canine "mansion" of twenty acres, equipped with splendid kennels, had been built on the shogunal estate at Ōkubo, in Edo. Among those who had helped build it was the governor of Kaga and Noto, the fabulously wealthy Lord Maeda. The commissioners in charge of construction were Lords Yonekura and Tō-dō, both illustrious liege lords themselves. The animals were handled with the greatest deference. Former falconers and bird-catchers were ordered out to comb the streets of Edo for stray dogs, which they were to catch —in the kindest possible way!—and bring to the "dog palace." Then the Law of Compassion for Fellow Creatures was passed, offenders were jailed or banished, and for grave offenses went to the gallows.

By now, Osugi was sitting curled up like a kitten beside Wabisuké, and sobbing quietly all through his story. Wabisuké recalled the number of stray dogs gathered at Ōkubo.

"It was something you'd never believe," he said, surprised all over again. "There were over a hundred thousand of them!"

Osugi covered her face with her hands once more. Wabisuké thought her "blood storm" might be reaching its climax, but he went on with his story.

"So . . . what was I saying? Jail or banishment—in Edo alone an amazing number of people were sentenced." Just recalling the figure made him angry. "It was terrible. Eight thousand people in one year's time!" Osugi burst into tears again. She covered her face and sobbed into her hands with a sucking sound, as if she were drinking, and her shoulders shook wildly. "Oh ... hoo ... hoo." To Wabisuké's eye, the storm in her body had reached high tide. It was like the frenzy of a woman wild drunk from too much saké. It didn't seem funny, nor yet make him sad. Strange to tell, it gave her a glowing charm, an almost smoldering quality.

"Oh yes," he said, touching his forehead, "and there was another one in Nakano. A dog palace, I mean. Next to the Ōkubo place. How big do you think it was? Nearly a hundred acres!" Osugi cried more fiercely. She had still only tasted her millet.

But Osugi's outburst had taken up too much time; he finished his business with the crows and led her down the mountain. They strolled along the village road looking out for sparrows to catch. Nothing was easier for Wabisuké. The tip of his fowling rod had to look like a single point to a sparrow's eye, and all he needed to do was keep it pointed straight at them. But catching them had been strictly prohibited until a few days ago. In fact, for the last ten years or so, the only way to keep down the crows and sparrows was to catch the nestlings and send them to a magistrate's office. Two years before, the birds had become such a nuisance the landowners of Kai had put their heads together and gone to the priest of a temple in Ichikawa Daimon for his sage advice. They first asked the bonze, could he sound out the magistrate for a permit to catch parent birds as well as their chicks? It's quite possible, they argued, to accustom old birds to taking feed in a cage, and there wasn't any specific regulation against *feeding* birds, was there? Feeling obliged to give the local magnates what assistance he could, the priest set off to convey their request. The magistrate was too angry to let him finish: was it only a rumor, or was his temple really a gambling den? Having no other choice, he went on to confer with the mother temple in Kōfu, to be told that success depended on how skillfully his petition was lodged and followed up. His advisers then laid out a master plan.

The Law of Compassion for Fellow Creatures was born of the fleeting whim of Chief Abbot Ryūkō, at the Temple of Holy Prayer in Edo; it swept through the shōgun's palace like a fever, and was solemnly adopted as a law of the land. This Ryūkō had originally been in charge of the

Sanctuary of Mercy at Hasedera temple in Yamato, having served his novitiate at the Shōdaiji in the same province. By great good luck, the man who had taught the esoteric chants of his sect to the abbot of the mother temple in Kōfu had served as superior of the same Shōdaiji thirty years before and was now retired and residing in Yamato, in a village called Nijō. To follow up this opportunity, the priest of Ichikawa Daimon first applied to the old anchorite at Nijō for a letter of introduction to the present superior of Shōdaiji temple, who gave him access to the abbot of Hasedera; through the abbot the present superior of the Sanctuary of Mercy was approached, and he finally got in direct touch with Chief Abbot Ryūkō in Edo on behalf of the Ichikawa Daimon priest's petitioners. By such roundabout routes was the petition presented. Besides serving the worthy cause of helping farmers get rid of flying pests, they had offered a token of their pious devotion to all the temples along the petition's route, so even if it came to nothing they would have the chief abbot's ear in the future. Ichikawa Daimon's temple as well as the mother temple of Kōfu would gain much face in the eyes of the magistrate of the area. Their petition might fail, but it did no harm to make friends with the oldest temples in Japan!

Meanwhile, the rich patrons of Ichikawa Daimon had to share the expense of these procedures. Each gave according to his year's yield of rent crops. At the head of the list came Ishihara, the local nabob of Toyotomi Village, with five hundred sacks of rice. Way down—almost falling off the list—was Jinsaku of Kunado Village, who could not give much: just seven sacks. His only distinction was to be Osugi's grandfather. But in the twentieth month after the petition was set in motion, and while it was still unanswered, official notice came that the law had been amended by one clause: if birds became an unbearable nuisance, and if farmers appealed for help, the government would consider sending someone to catch adult birds. The magistracy in Ichikawa Daimon indicated that this was the fruit of unstinting devotion to public duty on the part of all the petitioners, from the millionaire Ishihara on down to the worthy Jinsaku of the seven sacks. Which of course meant the magistracy was to be considered solely responsible for the added clause! The priest of the temple in Ichikawa Daimon, who loved playing go-between, ran busily back and forth between the magistracy and the landholders until it became clear they were expected to send *more* discreetly sealed bags, again according to the year's yield of their rent crops. They knew they couldn't turn back halfway along the road, so they grudgingly did as they were commanded. Only poor Jinsaku was left out in the cold. During the two years the petition was on its way, life for him and his house had become sheer misery. After fire had burned up his cherished mountain-side of cypress trees, Jinsaku died and left his granddaughter Osugi all alone. If that weren't enough, a heavy rain sweeping down the bare, blackened mountain had sent a landslide crashing into the river below, damming it up till the lake that formed was big enough to break through and wash away many fields in a flash flood. Though no lives—human or animal—had been lost, farmers with flooded fields had decided to hold the owner of the mountain responsible, and three or four of them sued Osugi for damages. Somebody even reported her for gross negligence, in abandoning the carcasses of some badgers just where they had been caught by the earlier fire. Osugi's trip to town with a little token of gratitude was thus no longer a matter of choice, although her house had signed the petition about the bird nuisance. Now she was summoned by the magistrate and interrogated as to the origins of the fire, and some constables were sent to investigate the scene. They found five dead badgers. The torrent had washed away enough ground to expose the roots of a large tree, and the five badgers curled beneath them. The fire must have roasted the animals in their den, and when the flood came and swept the soil away, it brought them to light. By this time the bodies were nothing but lumps of skin and bone at the bottom of a dried-out hollow; the wind blowing through their pelts had given them the look of silken floss, tanned to a dark brown in persimmon juice. They were found by a young man called Sanzō, one of the villagers guiding the constables (and the one who had informed against Osugi). He looked at the pelts and played it up a little for the others, stuffing them in his jacket and shouting: "Here's a find! I'll keep them and sell the long hairs to a writing-brush maker." But the constables arrested him on the spot and, though Sanzō's companions did their best to make excuses for him, roughly tied him up. For, according to the law—binding for all without exception— the carcasses of animals, even if killed under license, "must be buried as they are. They must on no account be used for meat, nor should they be flayed of their pelts. Any who contravene the above shall be liable to serious punishment. . . ." Furthermore, Sanzō had lifted important evidence from right under the noses of constables on an inspection tour! Wasn't this showing outright contempt for government officials? After tying him up, the constables dragged him around the scene of the fire, then down the mountain to a wayside shrine where they retied his bonds with stronger rope and gave him a sound flogging. Then they joined a long cord to the rope that held his hands behind him and threw it over the roof beam of the shrine. A husky-looking peasant was ordered to pull on the cord's end. Sanzō's arms were cruelly wrenched up behind his back, and as the pain grew the constable in charge growled, "Whenever you're ready. Let's have the whole story from the beginning!" Without much resistance, Sanzō began to babble of how he had courted Osugi and how she had brushed him off. To add to his shame, the whole village had turned out to gawk at him.

None of this was allowed to reduce Osugi's guilt one jot. Investigation into the fire was neglected, as was the increased danger from rain on the freshly denuded mountain. The question whether the landslide could have been prevented didn't matter so much as her flagrant carelessness: she hadn't even bothered to look over the site of the fire, and hence failed to report the animals' violent death. It was her own fault the infamy had come to light! To expose the corpses of a badger family to wind and weather on her hillside was a crime deserving death many times over, to say nothing of flood damage to the fields! However . . . since the culprit was of the fair sex, and in the springtime of life, without kith or kin, the judge would show exceptional clemency and merely banish her to Isle-on-the-Billows.

She had arrived on the island just a few days before. After hearing her story, Wabisuké thought, "So that's what it was! The girl had a 'bloodstorm' because she saw this burned-out wood."

As he sauntered about in no particular direction, holding out his fowling rod for sparrows, Wabisuké told Osugi about the bothersome rigmarole needed to convey sparrows and crows from one place to another—more bothersome for the birds than the people, he thought. After Wabisuké took the birds back to the Isle, they would be sent by courier to the magistracy at Ichikawa Daimon, to be watched over in relays, night and day, by three bird-catchers and half a dozen assistants till they were used to birdseed or ground paste. Then, with other birds born and raised in captivity, they would be ferried down the River Fuji with an escort to the aviary at Tagonoura, where they stayed for a while with birds from other places. From there they went to the post station at Numazu, before going by sea to Edo and its special aviaries. Four times yearly, together with birds captured within the city, they were loaded on an outgoing prison ferry bound for Hachijō, Miyaké, and Niijima islands, where they were set free for the first time. This was in no sense a "banishment" for the birds. A nuisance on the mainland, they were sent on a sort of "excursion" to a far island, where they could take up permanent residence in a thickly wooded paradise blessed with warm temperatures all the year round. No naughty children to tease them; no evil snakes to eat their eggs. It was no fairy tale, either: at this very moment, hawkers and fowlers were bringing nestlings down out of trees with all the care they could muster, as if handling the most fragile and valuable articles, rare as jewels. If they made a mistake and harmed a chick, their punishment would be draconian—a life, perhaps, for a life. If farmers were bothered by wild boar or rabbits, they weren't permitted to trap or shoot them. They could only chase them with noisemakers. If that didn't work, they could go to the magistrate, and after an affidavit was drawn up swearing them not to kill, they might fire blank shots to frighten away the game. Since most hill farmers couldn't read or write, they would take the local letter-writer with them to the magistrate's.

The farmers understandably envied dogs and birds their privileged position. As convicts on Hadakajima would say, in one of their work songs:

> I wish I could be
> A dog but I know
> It's too much for me
> To hope for, and so
>
> Perhaps if I die
> In heaven I'll be
> A bird in the sky
> And flying go free
>
> To kick my own eggs

Without any fear
Of feeling the lash
I keep getting here.

A heron behind's
As bald as his face.
If I was a feather
I'd fit into place!

Whenever the prisoners sang this tune, though, a guard was sure to turn up and rebuke its insolent parody of their ruler's wisdom. They were only permitted to sing aloud on the occasion of a fellow prisoner's obsequies, when they could intone the Nichiren prayer and "Buddha have mercy on us." Now, wanting to look bold in Osugi's eyes, Wabisuké said, "Listen—I'll sing you something," then, with bravado, "I don't give a hoot if the guard hears, either. Or the shōgun himself!" And he began to sing the work song. Though he kept it under his breath, he couldn't get the guards off his mind, and it came out like a sutra chanted at the bottom of a river. Osugi listened in mute fascination.

All in all, Wabisuké had "watched his step" that day, and both he and Osugi returned to the island. When he went to give back Tōkichi's money, the Gambler scratched his bull neck with a stubby finger and laughed. "I acted like a fool," he said, "but I had a feeling in the pit of my stomach you were up to something." Then he took back the coins.

The murmur of the river was melancholy as always. When the work crews had time, they would fish, but lately they'd been puzzled by the strange behavior of the trout. Once on the hook, they would pull down and dash away like lightning. You could tell by the pull on the rod they were heading right for the bottom. The slight earth tremors noticeable the last few days might have had something to do with it.

Wabisuké's next companion when he went bird-catching was not Osugi but a tall, ruddy-faced fat woman named Omon, from Ryūōmura— "Dragon King's Village." Still young and not bad-looking, she had a long stride and big feet with horn-like calloused toes that trod shoeless on thorny vines without discomfort. At first she had nothing to say. But after they'd left the ferry and taken to the village road, she announced, "They call me a loudmouth, but that's just the way I am," and began talking a blue streak. Her family used to spend half the year river fishing. Summers, they would move to the banks of the Kamanashi and use cormorants to catch trout. Then her father had died, and when her brother was away to work in Uenohara, she had a slapping match with the sister-in-law, who promptly went home to her family in another village. Her brother had a strong sense of duty toward his wife, and followed her to make his home there for good. There was no help for it: Omon had to do the farming and fishing by herself, until four years ago, when an official came from the magistracy at Isawa to confiscate her seven tame cormorants and take them back with him. Since the Law of Compassion for Fellow Creatures had been issued over a decade before, buying and selling meat or fish or eggs, let alone eating them, was forbidden. Luckily, from the time of the revered Takeda Shingen, Lord of Kai, her family had an appointment to keep their masters supplied with fresh trout. "The longer the lineage the deeper the bond," as the saying goes. Even the first great shōgun, Tokugawa Ieyasu, had thought twice about dropping ancient prerogatives given the province of Kai by its old lord. Who was *this* shōgun, after all the generations of his great patriarch's scions, to refuse to honor Omon's age-old family custom? His retainers, still less their local henchmen at the magistracy of Isawa, had no business interfering with her trained cormorants!

Without a word of warning, the official had descended on Omon with some litter bearers to stuff her precious birds, and with them her livelihood, into a cage.

Whether from anger at this outrage or from disbelief, Omon had for a moment been unable to speak. From the cupboard below her Buddhist altar, she drew out a family tree and showed it to the official, trying to explain the origins of the cormorant-fishing franchise that had been handed down to her. But he only said, "You'll have to plead your case before the magistrate." Omon saw that crying was her last resort and burst out with a loud wail, but not a muscle moved in the man's stern face. Seeing tears had no effect, she tried to compromise. "Since you say so, I'll stop fishing and just keep the birds. If I just let them loose, and feed them, I won't be breaking that law, will I?" And, with tears in her eyes, she begged him: "My cormorants have such weak wings, it's hard for them to pick up enough food along this rough coast. You

135

don't want them to suffer. Just this once, couldn't you overlook . . . ?"

The official spoke with conviction, if not much sense. "People who keep cormorants feed them fish and other live things, don't they? That's against the law. To heed the law means to love your country. If you love your country, no sacrifice is too great!" And he and his litter bearers went on their way with the cage.

When birds like cormorants are let loose, even on a rugged, desolate coast, they still look for live food. That night, Omon didn't sleep a wink thinking of it. It was the same the night after. The cormorants that had just been taken from her were used to seeing their mistress every day, and would greet her noisily when she came home. When she went out, their gaw-gawing calls yearned after her, begging to be taken along. They were as good as watchdogs, raising a shrill warning at the advent of strangers. All this was to be no more. Finally, she could stand it no longer, and set off for the Isawa magistracy determined to ask leave to say good-bye to her birds, even if she only got a glimpse of them. Permission was granted for a last visit. Omon smuggled in a bamboo tube full of loach and fed one to each of her cormorants. So heartbroken was she to part with them that, without thinking, she plucked a wing feather from Nightlight, her favorite pet. An officer of the magistracy happened to see this, and during the subsequent investigation and beating, the hidden tube was discovered, and she became a criminal despite herself. Not only had she maltreated the loach by squeezing them into a narrow tube, she had shortened their life by feeding them to her birds—a serious crime, not to speak of doing injury to a resident of the magistrate's zoo, right under the guard's nose!

Listening to Omon's chatter with one ear, Wabisuké walked along the path with the bird whistle in his mouth, imitating a sparrow's chirp. It looked like this one was working herself up to a "blood storm," too! He couldn't forget how Osugi had flung herself down to cry the day before, and almost looked forward to seeing the same kind of attractive glow on today's companion. Osugi had got all choked up when she came across the traces of a forest fire. What, he wondered, would get this woman choked up? Deciding to find out right away, Wabisuké asked her directly, "You're the kind that gets choked up easily, aren't you?"

The question was a bit unexpected, but Omon nodded hearty agree-

136

ment. "That's true. We young girls are like that. Mind you, I'm not as bad as Hatsutarō's old lady," she went on with zest. "When Hatsutarō's mother laps a little *miso* she gets choked up, too, the same when she eats rice so every mealtime you won't believe it but all she can eat is dry tea leaves, you should see her green face. . . ." She rattled on as if her tongue had wheels, all about this Hatsutarō's old mother, who had long been in service with an Ōsaka merchant family, and of what she had said and done and how chic she was. She could recite pages of fashionable Jōruri ballads, with heaven only knew how fine a cadence. ". . . As for that son of hers—he's just a gambler who plays all night and the *women* he chases after!" Only the need for breath made her halt for a moment.

They had come up to a hut by the roadside, and in a Chinese date tree growing next to it, a great flock of sparrows had gathered. Wabisuké blew softly on his whistle, trying not to frighten them off. Whenever he aimed his pole at some sparrows, it was a matter of interest to him how many he could catch in one thrust. At his first lesson in bird-catching, when he was still a boy, his teacher had shown him how to get five at one stroke. Wabisuké's record, on his best days, was four at once. Now, with Omon watching him, he managed to get three sparrows from the date tree the first time, and two more on his second thrust. The rest flew off.

"My heavens! That's amazing," said Omon in an awestruck voice. "If Hatsutarō could see that, now. . . ." Wabisuké wasn't listening any more. When they set off again through the rice paddies to the mountain path, Wabisuké blew his whistle all the way, to silence Omon's nattering.

From the direction of the new land-clearing, they could hear the sound of axes, mingled with the shouts of many men pulling together. With a last good-humored "Yo-heave-ho!" the shouting would stop, only to begin again a moment later on a less cheerful note. The two of them had toiled up along the stream to the ridge above the development site when they found a lone pine tree clinging to the rocky soil, with a nest on one of its branches. The trunk was thick and solid; fierce gales had twisted its limbs, yet still it stood, like a gnarled old veteran. He couldn't tell what kind of bird had made the nest. A cool wind was blowing. When he climbed up to investigate, it looked like a hawk's nest, but the young ones had left it some time before. After listening a moment to the moan of the wind through the pine needles, he slid down. Omon had already finished her lunch and was sitting beside the cage with her big feet thrown out in front of her.

Wabisuké opened his own lunch box. The odor of Omon's sweaty skin was different from Osugi's; something like the smell of a young nestling, only a little tangier. To a man's nose it was sweetness itself, and it put Wabisuké in a special, dreamy mood. After a while, he cleared his throat and began, "Did you know that the shōgun's dogs . . . eat two tons of rice every day? Along with ten barrels of *miso*, ten sacks of dried sardines, and fifty bundles of firewood to keep them warm. They even have a twenty-acre mansion of their own, at a place called Ōkubo." Here he paused, waiting for her surprise.

Omon gave a great yawn such as country people do after a good meal, and mumbled sleepily, "How'd you like to take a 'boat ride,' boss? I don't care if they do chop our heads off—just get me out of here!" She punctuated the dread words with a fart, but Wabisuké felt his blood turn to ice.

Omon lay on her side, head pillowed on one arm; half asleep already, she peered up at him through drowsy lids and said, "Don't think I'm just dreaming." Without lifting her head, she went on, "The shōgun's prob'ly with some dumb court lady now, someone with nothing to do but show off."

She had almost dozed off when she sat up to start another of her lively tales about something silly the Isawa magistracy had done.

Once they had issued a proclamation for a great crowd of farm girls from the nearby villages to muster at Isawa. An itemization of protocol for the occasion was sent to the headman of each hamlet:

> Item: Lord Yanagisawa, a most prominent personage among the higher officials at Edo, has been favored with another promotion.
>
> Item: Realizing what an unparalleled honor this is for the farmers of Kai, having as they do intimate ties with our noble patron, and in order to convey the full spirit of our joy at Lord Yanagisawa's elevation, we are sending a group of thirty farm girls from each village to the magistrate's seat.
>
> Item: All the young ladies are to wear their best clothes.

Item: They are to form a procession and march to Isawa in a live-ly, joyful fashion.

Item: On the way to Isawa, they will join with processions from other villages, at which time they will give three cheers of congratula-tion. Otherwise, they should stay silent and refrain from unseemly behavior.

Item: On arriving in front of the Isawa magistracy, they will line up together and again give three cheers.

Such was the notice. But even the farmers were aware of its real in-tention. The cheers were intended for Lord Yanagisawa's senior con-cubine, who was staying at the Isawa residency just then. It was to be no more than a little festive racketing, but the farmers weren't happy. Less than one in five of their daughters had suitable wear for the event. Even if they borrowed clothes, it was near the end of the frosty Eleventh Month and the few who could get hold of gala summer kimonos had nothing to wear underneath. The girls were much put out, trying one thing after another, but in the end they all turned out in their fathers' and brothers' crested *haori* overcoats.

Well, the great day came and the "chorus line" filed onto the riding course at the magistrate's residence; three clerks came running out to shepherd each village group through the gate by turns, and each group had its chance to stand under the veranda and shriek "Hip hip, hurray!" three times. The girls had all done their part, when who should come out to greet them? Not the magistrate, but the magistrate's wife in a kimono with a long train.

Everyone was shocked to see the mistress of the house saunter out at such a formal moment and just nod her head casually to the chorus of welcoming voices. It was quite contrary to good manners for the wife to leave the interior of the house. (Even nowadays no farm wife would dream of behaving in such a thoughtless manner.) The consensus was that the magistrate's wife was not only a fool but a terrible show-off as well.

Lord Yanagisawa's senior concubine was better behaved and kept to her room inside the house.

The points that Omon dwelt on in her story, about the borrowed clothes and the wife's showing off, are favorite subjects of gossip in Kai to this day—familiar to all except the very young.

Wabisuké had been standing for some time, shading his eyes and staring off into the distance, before he came to and realized Omon was talking to him. But he kept his gaze fixed on the horizon. It was the custom for anyone leaving the island with a pardon to turn around in the boat for a last glimpse of their "living Hell." So might Urashima Tarō, leaving the Dragon King's palace on a turtle's back, have turned for a last look at Princess Otohimé. Wabisuké held the same pose without thinking, but something more real than a legend lay before his eyes. He didn't especially *want* to look at that too well known island. In fact, the more he looked at the Isle, the more it disgusted him. There lay the parade ground with the lone pine tree; a horse had got loose and was careering around it. He could see fishermen standing atop the Mole of Hell by the ferry wharf. A little downriver, a solitary figure was driving some cattle across the ford. He had never noticed it before, but in the white poppy field by the cow barn bloomed a brilliant patch of red. . . .

That day, too, in keeping with his resolve to "watch his step," Wabisuké returned to the island in the evening, after spending the rest of the afternoon catching his quota of sparrows. Walking by the river that night, he came on the Gambler taking his bath, but neither of them felt like friendly conversation. One exile would sometimes speak to another in a close, chummy way; later, he might regret the burst of confidences and walk past his mate without seeing him. This time, Wabisuké simply threw some water over the Gambler's back to rinse him and withdrew with a terse "See you tomorrow."

Next day, almost the entire population of the colony was marched off to the work site on the mountainside and made to carry rocks from the river and build stone walls, to keep the soil of the newly manured and buckwheat-planted fields from washing away. (There were earth tremors all that year, almost daily from the First Month into summer. They were mild, but since the ground shook from ten to twenty times a day, many of the exiles on Hadaka had their relatives send proper talismans from the Asama Shrine. Some were even offered up on the little altar in the island's soup kitchen, but talk about earthquakes fell into the category of "wild rumor" and was banned absolutely; offenders were sent on their work details without lunch for three days running. This was such a nuisance for the exiles they stopped discussing earthquakes altogether. Work progressed unusually smoothly from then on, the days passing quietly, without incident.)

At the end of the Fifth Month of that year, the report from the magistracy said in part:

> From winter's end through spring, the prisoners on Hadakajima have been working on land reclamation. The work progresses well, and recently a good two and a half acres were opened up for new farms. In the spring months another acre was developed and secured against erosion by the construction of a stone wall.

But a calamity struck Hadaka that summer, in the Sixth Month—one of unprecedented proportions. A report delivered at year's end can be quoted in part:

> Since the First Month of this year, a succession of minor tremors has been observed, and people are spreading irresponsible rumors that Mt. Asama is going to erupt. On the afternoon of the fourth day of the Sixth Month, there was a major earthquake. . . . According to the later testimony of some inmates of Isle-on-the-Billows, it was during the same earthquake that the banks at the mouth of the Shimobé River, where it enters the Fuji, collapsed and the island of Hadaka began sliding downriver, in the next moment being swept away by the water. At the same time they saw great waves and waterspouts shooting past, and in their wake a high wind, carrying spray as far as the development site they were working on. The place they remembered the island to have been was now changed to a boundless torrent of blue water, too deep for the bottom to be seen; Isle-on-the-Billows had faded away, hidden by the gods. Along with it went Ono Hachirōemon, the warden, five guards and ferryboat captains, four trusties, male and female, and four convicts who had been confined because of illness. All these have disappeared without a trace. The 101 men engaged in hard labor in the fields were luckily spared, and eleven of them succeeded in a "boat escape." The remaining ninety having no place to go are in a hopeless situation,

as are the inhabitants of nearby farmhouses, who are likewise without shelter.

The great disaster struck in the afternoon, a little after four. When the prisoners who were still at work clearing new land on the hillside saw the Fuji River shrouded in spray, they froze in their tracks, unable to move or speak. By sheer chance, Wabisuké's eyes took in the scene seconds before the island slipped away. Then the river seemed to flow in reverse. In the same instant, the entire island turned into a whirling, snow-white waterspout. When it subsided, to be sucked smoothly back into the river, the island was no more. All that could be seen were high waves washing the river's banks. For a fleeting moment, Wabisuké's eyes held a deep imprint of the red poppies he'd glimpsed before the island went down. Somewhere nearby he heard cries for help: "I can't keep my feet! The ground won't stay still!" and when he looked he saw the prisoner who had called, as well as Osugi, sprawled on the ground.

After the surging waves in the river settled down, all that remained was a wide, smooth expanse of water; without the island, the landscape looked broken and empty.

Notes on "Waves: A War Diary"

(With the exception of self-explanatory names, all persons and places not accounted for in maps or notes are fictional.)

Page 26   **Harada, Kikuchi, and Matsura**
Heiké retainers from among the local gentry of southwestern Japan. This is a paraphrase of the opening lines of Chap. XIII, Book 7, of the *Heiké monogatari*. Kitagawa and Tsuchida give the last as "Matsuura."

Lord Yorimori's residence here in the Rokuhara
In Japanese, simply *Rokuhara ikedono*, or "the Ikedono mansion of Rokuhara." Rokuhara was the main Heiké estate in Kyōto, consisting of many separate pavilions and residences. Ikedono was the mansion of Taira no Yorimori (1132–86), youngest brother of the former clan patriarch, Kiyomori (see note for page 44).

eagle's-feather fletchings
Arrows were not only weapons but heraldic accessories to a samurai's outfit. The ornamental fletchings often signified military or personal rank.

trapped in a valley in Etchū
A reference to the Kurikara Pass in Etchū, or modern Toyama Prefecture, where the Heiké suffered a major defeat.

Page 27   **General Shigehira**
His rank is *sanmi chūjō* in the text—usually translated as "Lieutenant General," but we preferred the shorter "General" as more appropriate to a loosely organized medieval army. Taira no Shigehira (1156–85) was the youngest son of Kiyomori and the brother of our hero's father, Tomomori.

Kiso
Minamoto no Yoshinaka (1154–84), a Genji general famous for his

bravery and brutal temper. During the paramountcy of the Heiké, he was exiled to Kiso, a mountainous region of Shinano Province, and later adopted it for a surname. Although he was cousin to the Genji leaders Yoritomo and Yoshitsuné, he was destroyed by his own clansmen.

the young emperor
At that point there were two emperors: the "cloistered" or "ex-emperor" Goshirakawa, and the young emperor Antoku (see note for page 32), whose accession to the throne in 1180 made Taira no Kiyomori the "imperial grandfather."

Seno-o
That is, Seno-o no Kaneyasu, a provincial nobleman from Bitchū (now Okayama) who was a loyal vassal of Kiyomori.

East Sakamoto
A village on the shore of Lake Biwa, in the old province of Ōmi. It lay at the foot of Mt. Hiei (see following note) on a road going up the mountain.

Mt. Hiei
A mountain 2,781 ft. in height, lying on the border between the prefectures of Kyōto and Shiga, northeast of the city of Kyōto. A place of religious veneration since prehistoric times, in the early Heian period it became the site of Enryakuji, the central temple of the Tendai sect of Japanese Buddhism. By the time of our story, there was a large fortified monastery there with thousands of warrior-monks (*sōhei*), fully armed and trained in the military arts. The capital had often been menaced by this sectarian army.

Omi
Most probably in modern Yamagata Prefecture, near the town of Matsuyama, at the confluence of the Mogami and Aisawa rivers.

Aida
A village located in what is now Higashi Chikuma County in Nagano Prefecture.

Kurosaka
On the way from Mt. Tonami to the Kurikara Pass (see note for page 26: Etchū).

Page 28   **the Hōgen business**
The first clash between the Heiké and the Genji took place in the

first year of the Hōgen period (1156–58). The Heiké were victorious and Kiyomori rose to power.

Hachijō silk
A type of fine silk produced on Hachijōjima, one of the Seven Isles of Izu. See map on page 7 and our second story, "Isle-on-the-Billows," where it is mentioned as the location of a penal colony.

tassets
The two plates of armor hanging in front over the groin, known as *kusazuri* in Japanese. Originally a French word, as is most such terminology.

Page 29 **Vice-Councillor Tomomori**
Taira no Tomomori (1152–85) was the third son of Kiyomori and the father of our hero, Tomoakira. His court rank was Junior Grade of the Second Rank and his full title, New Vice-Councillor and Commander in Chief against the Barbarians. He died at Dannoura, in the decisive naval battle of the Genji–Heiké war.

Page 30 **a temple at Uzumasa**
That is, at the temple of Kōryūji in the Ukyō Ward of Kyōto.

Third Avenue
Originally modeled on the geometrical plan of cities in classical China, Kyōto was laid out in horizontal "avenues" and vertical "streets" (the reverse of the New York system). Gradually, entire districts came to be called after the nearest avenue, Sanjō or Rokujō, for example. We used the term to suggest a large, well-organized city.

fragrant orchid
Japanese *fūran* (*Neofinetia Falcata Hu*), a small parasite orchid of the Anglecum group originally from Africa. Unlike the more gorgeous tropical orchids, it has narrow little blade-shaped leaves, modest but elegant white blossoms, and a fine fragrance.

nagi tree
An evergreen (*Pennisetum Japonicum*) which grows in warm, southern climates to about fifty feet. Its narrow, shiny leaves are quite hardy and in summer it produces small, light yellow blossoms. The finely textured wood is used for ornamental alcove posts, etc., and twigs of leaves (which resemble those of bamboo) were used in the old days as talismans.

Suzaku Gate
The main central gate on the south side of the Imperial Palace—one

of the twelve surrounding it—was entered from the so-called Suzaku Ōji (Main Street).

Page 31 **lord chamberlain**
Originally *shūri daibu*, or "chief of the Palace Repairs Division." The incumbent of this court sinecure was Taira no Tsunemori—another of Kiyomori's brothers. As he functioned as a chamberlain for the empress dowager, we used this shorter and more appropriate title.

Page 32 **Ex-Emperor Goshirakawa**
In the original, *hō-ō*, literally "Cloistered Emperor." In 1158, Goshirakawa (1127–92), the second of this name, had followed the practice of abdication—to avoid tiring ceremonial—and retirement as a Buddhist "monk." But he was still emperor de facto, and tried (unsuccessfully) to maintain the traditional imperial role against the impending dictatorship of the samurai. He is remembered as a wily schemer and opportunist.

Emperor Antoku
The six-year-old son of the previous emperor, Takakura. He ascended to the throne in 1180 at the age of two, and the real power was wielded by his mother's father, Taira no Kiyomori (see note for page 44). He was drowned at Dannoura in 1185.

the former minister Munemori
This was Taira no Munemori (1147–85), Kiyomori's second son and the Heiké commander in chief. Shigemori, his capable elder brother, died before the conflict reached its climax, leaving the uninspired Munemori with the highest title—Junior Grade of the First Rank— to succeed to his military duties.

Komatsu estate
This belonged to Taira no Shigemori and was situated in the present Higashiyama Ward of Kyōto.

Shirakawa
A district of Kyōto, on the east Kamo River, now known as Sakyō Ward.

Fukuhara
Taira no Kiyomori had tried to establish a new capital for his protégé Antoku on the site of his retreat at Fukuhara—where Kōbé is today— but conservative opposition brought it back to Kyōto.

Page 33 **old palace**
That is, the palace established for Emperor Antoku in the temporary

capital of Fukuhara.

Page 34   **Narizumi**
In the original, this was Narizumi Saburō, but since there are so many similar given names like Saburō and Shirō, not to mention Saburōji, Saburōbyōé, Shirōji, etc., in our text, we have tried to avoid confusion by using the more distinctive part of the names whenever possible.

Page 36   **chief councillor of Uji**
Or in Japanese, *Uji dainagon*. The offices of the *dajōdaikan* (Chief Council of State) were as follows:
First rank: 1. The *daijō*—(or *dajō*)—*daijin* (grand councillor of state or premier) was at the top with three ministers under him.
Second rank: 2. *Sadaijin* (minister of the left). 3. *Udaijin* (minister of the right). 4. *Naidaijin* (minister of the center).
Third rank: 5. *Dainagon* (chief councillor of state). 6. *Chūnagon* (vice-councillor of state).
Our hero's father filled this last position.

Tomonotsu
Older Japanese editions of this story, including Ibuse's *Collected Works*, give this name as Muronotsu. But in the latest Sakuhinsha edition, the author has changed the fictional one to Tomonotsu, close to the real name of a fishing port on the Inland Sea, Tomonoura. It is near Fukuyama in Hiroshima Prefecture, where Ibuse went to school.

Page 38   **Bugaku dance**
A masked dance with music, and together with Gagaku the most ancient form of Japanese music, originating in China.

Page 39   ***karatachi* hedge**
Citrus trifoliata, a tough, thorny bush known variously in English as Bengal quince or trifoliate orange.

Page 42   **Sasa-no-semari**
The Tale of the Heiké (Chap. VIII, Book 8. "The Death of Seno-o no Kaneyasu," p. 485) only says "Kaneyasu's fortress near Fukuryūji-nawate in Bizen"; it follows from the context that Sasa-no-semari may refer to the same fortress, since it is mentioned elsewhere (in Chap. X, Book 8. "Captain Tsuzumi") in Kiso's boastful speech.

Page 43   ***kosode***
A short-sleeved robe for everyday use, forerunner of today's kimono.

Page 44   **Some minister of protocol's upstart young brother**

Or in Japanese, *nakatsukasakyō no goshatei*: literally, "the honorable younger brother of the minister of central affairs."

our late Lord Kiyomori
Grand Councillor Taira no Kiyomori (1118–81), patriarch of the Heiké clan and chief architect of its power, died before the opening of our story, but his shadow looms large, as it does to this day in history and legend. After his original defeat of the Genji, he took Lady Tokiwa, widow of Yoshitomo (see note for page 74), as his mistress and spared her sons Yoritomo and Yoshitsuné, who were eventually to exterminate his clan.

A man of strong appetites and fierce temper, he died of a mysterious disease that made his body radiate heat "like a burning fire," as in the satirical poem:

> "Monk" Kiyomori shouts
> "Bring chilled women,
>   Chilled women!"

He appears as a major character in Yoshikawa Eiji's historical novel *The Heiké Story* (Knopf, 1956).

Page 46   **One of the senior officers**
Literally *sachūjō*, or lieutenant general of the left. This was Taira no Kiyotsuné, third son of Shigemori.

Pure Land teachings
Refers to the Jōdo sect of Buddhism. Its founder Hōnen stressed the chanting of sutras as the sole avenue to salvation.

Atsumori
The Japanese here only mentions "the youngest son of the lord chamberlain." But since Taira no Tsunemori's youngest son is the beautiful courtier and accomplished flute player killed by Kumagai no Naozané in a famous encounter at Ichinotani, and the most popular tragic hero from the Heiké epic, we use his given name. The Japanese reader would, of course, know whom Ibuse is referring to.

Page 52   **Heiji battles**
A reference to the so-called Heiji incident (*Heiji no ran*) in 1159. It was the second unsuccessful Genji attempt to overthrow the Taira hegemony. The Genji forces were led by Minamoto no Yoshitomo (see note for page 74).

the rebel emperor Sutoku
In the original, *shin'in*, or "new cloistered emperor." In 1124, Cloistered Emperor Toba abdicated in favor of his first son, Sutoku.

But after Toba's consort had given him another son in 1139, he made him crown prince and in 1141 placed him on the throne, planning to rule as regent. Consequently, the deposed Sutoku—now the new cloistered emperor—rebelled in 1150 with the support of Genji forces.

the Yoshitomo affair
That is, the Heiji incident. See note above (Heiji battles).

Minamoto no Tametomo
Or as the Japanese text has it, Tsukushi no Hachirō, a sobriquet meaning "Hachirō of Kyūshū" from the place where he gained his military fame. Minamoto no Tametomo (1139–70), eighth son of Minamoto no Tameyoshi, was one of the fiercest warriors of the Genji clan with a great reputation for his archery.

Page 53   **Itōroku . . . Itōgo**
Both these names appear in the *Hōgen monogatari* (see W. Wilson's translation), of which this passage is a close paraphrase. By including it, Ibuse suggests that Kakutan either is quoting an early version of the Hōgen epic, or that he might have written it himself. In actual fact, the anonymous authors of such *gunki monogatari* must have been erudite monks of Kakutan's type.

pauldrons
Simply *sode* or "sleeves" in Japanese, actually pieces of armor hanging from the shoulder, similar to the pauldrons or épaulières of Western knights. Consisting of layers of metal slats woven together with cord, Japanese armor was designed to stop arrows by "catching" them.

a turnip-shaped 'howler'
A *kaburaya* was a type of arrow with a round, turnip-shaped head, in which holes were pierced to make a siren-like noise to intimidate the enemy, or as a signal.

Ōba Heita
From the same passage of the *Hōgen monogatari* as Itōroku and Itōgo above.

Page 54   **the Law of our Lord Buddha**
Kakutan is referring to the esoteric rituals of Shingon (True Word), a rival sect; yet he is equally skeptical of the "Law" of his own Tendai (named after the monastery of T'ien-t'ai in China).

Prince Takahira . . . is to be called Gotoba
Literally *shi no miya*, or Fourth Prince. The fourth son of Emperor

Takakura, Gotoba (1180–1239) later attempted to challenge the Kamakura government and restore his imperial power. He was banished to the islands of Oki for his pains.

Page 55 the West Country
Because the Japanese islands form a reverse S curve, it is not always clear what area is meant. "North" is the upper part of Honshū and "east" its outer curve halfway down. "West" takes in the rest of the main island, plus Shikoku, while the "south" is Kyūshū.

the Hokuriku prince
One of Goshirakawa's grandsons, lived 1165–1230.

the Fujiwara of the north
The most powerful family in Japan (up to this time) was the Fujiwara, which was divided into several local houses. The most remote from Kyōto was Fujiwara Hidehira's military establishment in Hiraizumi. At different periods, he gave Yoshitsuné sanctuary from the boy's two dangerous enemies—the Heiké leader Kiyomori and his own brother Yoritomo! At this point, Goshirakawa and the Heiké leaders were trying to enlist him in the fight against Yoritomo. Hidehira wisely ignored them. A mandate to attack Kiso was never offered him.

the Latter Days of the Law
A common belief of the day held that with the Buddha gone from it, the world would be plunged into darkness and decay.

Chief Councillor Tokitada, his cousin the director of the storehouse, and his son the governor of Sanuki
The director of the storehouse was Nobumoto, and the governor of Sanuki, Tokizané. They were "spared disgrace" first because Goshirakawa was negotiating through Tokitada for the return of Antoku and his regalia, and, second, because the ex-emperor was married to Tokitada's sister, which gave his entire family privileged treatment.

Page 56 Saga and Ōhara
Villages on the outskirts of Kyōto. Now part of the city.

Usuki, Hetsugi
Initially these were Heiké allies like the others (who are mentioned on page 26), but later they were to turn against them. Their names appear three or four times in the *Heiké monogatari*.

the new lieutenant general, Sukemori
The second son of Shigemori, and like most men of the "Komatsu

152

house" an incompetent commander. He died in 1185.

Page 57 **Bishop Eryō**
Although there is a contemporary Bishop Eryō in *The Tale of the Heiké*, Kakutan slyly suggests he knew the earlier Eryō (801–60), a sage and ascetic of the early Tendai sect.

Itsukushima Shrine
Innumerable pictures of its big main *torii* gate out in the water have made this, in Western eyes, Japan's most famous shrine—though few know its name. It lies on the island of Miyajima, opposite Hiroshima. Incidentally, it is nowhere near Mt. Fuji, with which it is sometimes shown.

Tamanoura
There is an ancient port of the same name in northern Shikoku, but Ibuse locates it on the coast opposite Onomichi, so it is presumably fictional.

Page 58 **Minamoto no Yukiié**
This was the tenth son (?–1186) of Minamoto no Tameyoshi, and the uncle of Kiso Yoshinaka. In the original text, he is given the title *kurando*, corresponding to "keeper of the privy seal" or "imperial secretary."

Page 59 **Michisuké was deputy governor of Nagato**
Ibuse gives his title as "deputy chief of the Judicial Affairs Division." We have used another of his titles more relevant to the story.

Page 61 **Yasumitsu of Kamo**
This is possibly the Kamo district of Kyōto. Kamo is also the name of the author's home village, but there is no such historical person.

Po Chü-i
One of the greatest poets in Chinese literature (772–846). Arthur Waley has translated him extensively, and written a biography.

Page 62 **Kiyomuné, a captain of the palace guards**
Taira no Kiyomuné, son of Munemori, commander in chief of the Heiké.

my little niece Rokudai
There is a *boy* called Rokudai in the *Heiké monogatari*, younger than our hero. Although the Sakuhinsha edition of "Waves" gives *toshiue no mei* (older niece), the context suggests it is a printing error, and we follow Ibuse's *Collected Works* here.

153

Fujiwara Yoritsuné, son of Lord High Marshal Yorisuké
See *The Tale of the Heiké*, Chap. III, Book 8, pp. 468–69: "At that time the province of Bungo was the fief of Lord High Marshal Yorisuke. Having remained in the capital, he had sent his son, Yoritsune, to be his subordinate in that province. Now Yoritsune received a letter from his father. . . ." The letter orders Yoritsuné to unite his warriors and expel the Heiké from Kyūshū. (Kitagawa and Tsuchida translation, Univ. of Tokyo, 1975.)

a bandit chief of uncertain pedigree
His name, Ogata no Saburō, is left out here. *The Tale of the Heiké*, Chap. III, Book 8, explains his "uncertain pedigree": he was the descendant of a monstrous serpent, said to be the incarnation of a local deity. Hence his "power."

Yanagigaura
Now part of the city of Nagasu in Ōita Prefecture, northeastern Kyūshū.

Lt. General of the Left Kiyotsuné
Taira no Kiyotsuné (?–1183), the third son of Shigemori (see note for page 73).

Mt. Tekkai
One of the mountains forming the valley of Ichinotani, where the crucial battle in our story takes place. Other mountains in the area are Mt. Rokkō, Mt. Takatori, and Mt. Hachibusé near the village of Suma, on the outskirts of modern Kōbé.

"Genryaku"
The beginning of Emperor Gotoba's reign is disputed. Japanese dictionaries give variously 1183 or 1184. See note for page 71.

Noriyori
This was Minamoto no Noriyori (?–1193), stepbrother to Yoritomo and Yoshitsuné, called "the cadet of Gama" in the text. He helped to crush Yoshinaka and pursued the remnants of the Heiké army to Kyūshū. He attempted to appease Yoritomo after his falling-out with Yoshitsuné, but without success, and he was killed at the Shūzenji temple in Izu.

Kobata
Now part of Uji in the urban district of Kyōto.

Hachijō
"Eighth Avenue" in Kyōto, and by extension the Eighth Ward. (See

note for page 30.)

Fushimi
Presently one of the wards of Kyōto, in the southern part.

Nagasaka Pass
On the old Tamba High Road. (See page 75.)

Awataguchi
Located in Sakyō Ward of modern Kyōto.

five doughty warriors
The names of Hatakeyama no Jirō, Shibuya no Kōtarō, Sasaki no Shirō, Kajiwara no Genta, and Yasuda no Saburō have been omitted here, as they have little bearing on the story.

Kanehira
Imai no Shirō Kanehira was the foster brother of Kiso Yoshinaka.

Kugo Shallows
Off Tanakami, at the southern end of Ōtsu City.

Page 70 **Awazu**
Awazugahara, in the modern prefecture of Shiga.

Imai Kanetō
Also known as Kiso Kanetō, dates unknown. When Kiso Yoshinaka's father was killed in battle, his mother left her little son in Kanetō's care.

Page 71 **I want to write . . . Juei**
The name of the era had changed on the accession of Emperor Gotoba, signifying the rise of Genji power and the decline of the Heiké.

Itayado
Now in the Suma district of Kōbé.

Takasago
A city in the southern part of Hyōgo Prefecture. It has been a harbor town since ancient times and became famous mainly through the Nō play *Takasago*. The central image of this play—the twin pines of Takasago—is one of the best-known clichés of classical poetry. These trees grow in the precincts of the local Shintō shrine.

Page 72 **governor of Noto**
Taira no Noritsuné (1160–85) was the son of Kiyomori's younger

brother Norimori and the only able commander of all his relations.

pirate bands
Japanese "pirates" were not quite the wild outlaws we usually picture in the West. In fact, the word used for them here is *suigun*, which now means "navy." They resembled the well-organized semiofficial forces of Drake, Raleigh, and Henry Morgan. They held permanent strongholds in the Inland Sea, from which they issued to collect protection money or to ally themselves with warring daimyōs. They could make or break even aspiring shōguns, so perhaps "privateer" is a more suitable word.

Page 73 **Shigemori**
Taira no Shigemori (1138–79), eldest son of clan patriarch Kiyomori, was the most skillful and prudent politician among the Heiké leaders. Neither too rash nor too hesitant, he would have been an asset in the final confrontation with the Genji, but unfortunately died beforehand.

Mt. Takatori
See note for page 68.

Page 74 **Yoshitomo**
Minamoto no Yoshitomo (1123–60), stable master of the left, fought for Goshirakawa in the Hōgen incident and started the Heiji riot. He was later executed as a "traitor" by the victorious Heiké. His sons Yoritomo and Yoshitsuné justified their last attack on the Heiké as a revenge for their dead father.

Genta the Wicked
Minamoto no Yoshihira (1140–60), eldest son of Yoshitomo. He acquired his nickname "Akugenta" at the age of fifteen, after killing his uncle and defecting from his army. He was captured and sentenced to death by the Heiké, but a legend says he took the form of the Thunder God and destroyed his executioner with a bolt of lightning.

Page 75 **Shimohata, Taibata**
Villages along the Tamba High Road.

I have heard that in battle
Kakutan reads from a Japanese translation of the classic Chinese military strategist Sun-tze (c. 300 B.C.).

Page 76 **Wang Wei**
The great painter-poet (669–759) of the T'ang who supposedly

created the "southern" style of landscape composition. A good representation of his poems can be found in Bynner and Kiang's *Jade Mountain* anthology.

Page 77 **Inamino**
An old name for Hyōgo Prefecture.

Page 78 **Ikuno road**
One of the old "high roads" of present-day Hyōgo Prefecture, connecting the Sanyō and Sanin areas.

hirumaki sword
Literally "leech-wrapped" sword: the hilt and sheath are wrapped spirally with a thin strip of tanned leather or other material, giving the effect of coiled leeches.

Page 79 **Chinese philosophy and astrology**
Ibuse says *inyōgaku to tenmon*, literally "divination and astrology," but we wanted to give a sense of how seriously these disciplines were taken.

Page 81 **Major General Arimori**
Taira no Arimori was the fourth son of Shigemori.

Tadafusa, the chamberlain of Tango
Taira no Tadafusa was the sixth son of Shigemori, and younger brother to Sukemori. It should be remembered that aristocratic males might have several consorts (official and unofficial) and that "brothers" would often be raised in separate households.

governor of Bitchū
This was Taira no Moromori, fifth and youngest son of Shigemori. He was killed at Ichinotani.

Inagé
Inagé Shigenari (?–1205) was of the Oyamada family, son of Arishigé.

Toi
Or as some give it, Doi. Toi Sanehira was an old ally of Yoritomo, and a famous warrior.

Sahara
Sahara Yoshitsura's dates of birth and death are unknown. He was from the Miura family, and a son of Yoshiaki.

Kumagai
The fame of Kumagai no Naozané (?–1208) rests on his remorse at having killed the beautiful young Heiké warrior Atsumori (see note for page 46). He had originally fought *against* the Genji.

Page 82 **governor of Echizen**
This was Taira no Michimori, elder brother of the capable Noritsuné, governor of Noto (see note for page 72).

governors of Satsuma, Tajima, and Wakasa
Taira no Tadanori, Taira no Tsunemasa, and Taira no Tsunetoshi. Tadanori (1144–84) was the younger brother of Kiyomori, and died at Ichinotani.

Page 85 **Kajiwara Heiza**
A famous Genji warrior (?–1200) from Sagami. "Heiza" was his nickname, Kagetoki his given name. This passage is a close paraphrase of one in the *Heiké monogatari*.

Gongorō Kagemasa
Kajiwara's ancestor, whose dates are unknown. He was a retainer of one of the great Minamoto leaders, Minamoto no Yoshiié (see below).

Hachiman-tarō Yoshiié
Minamoto no Yoshiié (1041–1108) was nicknamed "Hachiman-tarō" (the War God's son) for his legendary military exploits. Hachiman was almost the "patron saint" of the Minamoto.

Kanazawa Castle in Dewa
Kanazawa is on the west coast of Honshū, where we have marked Kaga. Dewa originally took up most of northwest Honshū.

Page 87 **River Karumo**
A stream which now runs through the city of Kōbé.

Page 89 **Lord Moritoshi**
Taira no Moritoshi (?–1184) was a kinsman of Kiyomori. His title was governor of Etchū. See Chap. XIII of the *Heiké monogatari*, "The Death of Moritoshi."

Inomata no Koheiroku
Also called Inomata Noritsuna, dates unknown. He also appears in Chap. XIII of the *Heiké monogatari*.

Page 90 **Narimori**
Taira no Narimori (?–1184) was the third son of Taira no Norimori.

the still untitled Tsunetoshi
That is, he has no *court* title, but is the governor of Wakasa (see note for page 82).

Yasuda Yoshisada
Related to the Takeda family of Kai. He played a major part in the Genji victory, but Yoritomo turned against him and he was killed in 1194.

Sanyō High Road
An old highway connecting the provinces along the Inland Sea. It ran from eastern Harima through Bizen and Bitchū to western Aki, Suō, and Nagato.

Page 91 **chief councillor**
This was the Taira no Tokitada (1127–89) first mentioned on page 55. One of the major political figures of the time, he was captured at Dannoura and sent into exile in Noto by Yoritomo.

Page 93 **Takiguchi**
Takiguchi was originally the name of one of the Imperial Palace buildings, which came to be associated with individuals fulfilling a court function.

Page 95 **Gongorō**
There is no connection here with the Gongorō Kagemasa of page 85.

Samigahama
Most likely present-day Samihama in Okayama Prefecture, near the city of Kurashiki.

Page 96 **In defeat, we have still our mountains**
A paraphrase of Bashō's *Narrow Road to the Deep North* in the description of the ruins of Takadate Fort. Bashō in turn is quoting the T'ang poet Tu Fu. The last sentence, ". . . announcing the cruel law . . . ," echoes *The Tale of the Heiké.*

the burning of the Rokuhara
Here again Ibuse follows the descriptions in the *gunki monogatari* (Heiji and Hōgen) quite closely, suggesting that their anonymous authors were probably literate monks of Kakutan's type.

Funasaka Pass
A pass between the old provinces of Harima and Bizen, connecting the modern towns of Kamigōri in Hyōgo Prefecture and Mitsuishi in Okayama Prefecture.

Page 97 **Minister of the Right Kanezané**
Fujiwara Kanezané or Kujō no Kanezané (1149–1207) held various
official posts before becoming regent and later chief adviser to the
emperor. He was a calligrapher and waka poet of some note, and wrote
a diary called the *Gyokuyō*.

chief imperial adviser
In Japanese, *kampakuin*. An important, if somewhat obscure, government post that existed from the late ninth century until Meiji.

Muromachi district
A quarter of Kyōto where the Ashikaga shōguns later resided, so giving its name to the Muromachi period (1392–1573).

mistakenly inscribed with my own name
In fact, the historical Tomoakira saved his father's life at Ichinotani
and was killed himself.

Page 98 **Lord High Chamberlain Naritada**
Taira no Naritada (1160–1212). His Japanese title means literally
"Chief of the (Bureau) of Imperial Cuisine."

northern palace
A poetic reference to the Imperial Palace in Kyōto (as distinct from
the young emperor Antoku's present residence in the south).

Tōdaiji
One of the oldest and grandest temples of Japanese Buddhism, built
in 745–52 to house the great bronze Buddha of Nara. After its
monks declared for the Genji, the Heiké commander Shigehira burned
it down in 1180. The victorious Genji immediately rebuilt it. It was
again burned down in the mid-sixteenth century and restored on a
reduced scale around 1700.

Southern Ocean
A passage of considerable obscurity. It may be a reference to a Chi-
nese poem cycle from the third century B.C., the *Chiu Chang* (Nine
Declarations):

> 23. There is a bird from the South Country come to settle north
> of the Han;
> 24. Most fair and rare and beautiful, . . . Forlorn he sits in this
> foreign land,
> 25. Alone and cut off from the rest of the flock, With no one
> by to find him a mate.

(David Hawkes, from *Ch'u Tz'u: The Songs of the South*, Oxford, 1959.)

Kangaku Academy
The Kangaku was an elite school established in Kyōto at the beginning of the Heian period (794–1185) by the Fujiwara regents.

Page 99 **The ex-emperor's secretary**
This is a simplification of "Chief of the Palace Repairs Division Chikafusa."

Page 100 **Kuninobu**
The lord of Tosa, a historical personality mentioned in the *Azuma kagami*, but no details are given.

Narizumi
Not the Narizumi of page 34. He appears as "Narizumi of Kaga Province" in Chaps. VI, Book 7, and VIII, Book 8, of *The Tale of the Heiké*. He is the one who takes Seno-o no Kaneyasu alive at Kurikara.

Mitsuishi
A popular stop for travelers along the old Sanyō road, on the border of Hyōgo and Okayama prefectures, at the foot of the western slope of the Funasaka Pass.

Fukurinji-nawaté
This same episode is described in Chap. VIII, Book 8, of *The Tale of the Heiké*, but the place is called Fukuryūji-nawate. It is at the north end of the modern city of Okayama.

Ihara
There is an Ibara in the southern part of Shizuki County, Okayama Prefecture, but this is perhaps too far west for fugitives to reach from Fukurinji.

Page 102 **Sotoura**
A part of Kōnoshima is still called Sotoura.

Notes on "Isle-on-the-Billows"

Page 115 **Kai**
Used throughout this translation for the old province (also called Kō-shū in the original text) and for modern Yamanashi Prefecture. Formerly the domain of the sixteenth-century warlord Takeda Shingen.

hot springs
A small spa, called Yunomachi, on the Shimobé River.

Law of Compassion for Fellow Creatures
Or in Japanese, *shōrui awaremi no rei*, a law passed in 1687 by the fifth Tokugawa shōgun, Tsunayoshi. It was suggested by his religious adviser, Ryūkō, as an enforcement of the Buddhist concept of compassion for all living things. It forbade the buying and selling of fish or fowl, and actually prescribed capital punishment for anyone who mistreated dogs. See note for page 127: "the shōgun . . . his kennels." Although the situation described in this story may seem satirically exaggerated, it largely corresponds to historical reality.

Hachijōjima, Miyakejima, or Niijima
These are three of the so-called Seven Isles of Izu, lying southeast off the coast of the Izu Peninsula. These islands were used as penal colonies because of their distance from Edo, but they were directly under the city's jurisdiction.

Page 116 **"the outside world"**
In Japanese, *shaba* (from Sanskrit *sahā*), a Buddhist term meaning "this world." Here it is used in its slang sense—common in barrack, prison, and gay quarters like the Yoshiwara—of "civvy street."

Page 117 **Ido house**
Lord Ido was one of the direct retainers of the shōgun, and received

a yearly stipend of 2500 *koku* of rice. His family was originally from Yamato.

Yanagisawa Yoshiyasu
Lived 1658–1714. A favorite vassal of Shōgun Tsunayoshi, who became a senior councillor (*rōjū*) in his cabinet, and in 1704 was granted the 15,000 *koku* fief of Kōfu (see map) in Kai. He was popularly supposed to have corrupted Tsunayoshi by pandering to his weaknesses and was in fact dismissed after the shōgun's death. There is a Kabuki play based on the lurid legend that he had planned to poison Tsunayoshi but was forestalled by the shōgun's consort, Osaméno-kata, who stabbed Yanagisawa and then committed suicide.

shōgun
See note for page 127.

Page 118 **hayashi orchestra**
A traditional ensemble, basically of big and small drums, flute, gong, and shamisen. It was used, with variations, for the accompaniment of *nagauta* recitals, Nō, Kabuki, and other theatrical performances.

Page 125 **Kōfu**
Capital city of Kai, and now of Yamanashi Prefecture. In the sixteenth century it was the stronghold of Takeda Shingen. Its population is now about 125,000.

Mt. Minobu
It is here that the main monastery of the Nichiren sect and the temple of Kuonji (also called the Minobusan Myōhō Rengein) are located. In 1706—about the time of this story—it became a *chokugansho*, or "Sanctuary for Imperial Prayers."

Page 127 **the shōgun . . . his kennels**
The shōgun at the time of the story was Tsunayoshi (1646–1709), the fifth of the Tokugawa line—a cultivated man who ruled well in the first years of his career, depending on the wise counsel of his senior minister, Hotta Masayoshi. After Hotta's death, Tsunayoshi's favorite, Yanagisawa Yoshiyasu (see note for page 117), usurped his power, and financial policy fell into the hands of the accounts commissioner, Ogiwara Shigehidé, who boosted land taxes, debased the currency, and created economic havoc in the course of enriching himself. The shōgun, meanwhile, gave himself up to luxurious living and indulgence in increasingly eccentric projects. One of these—his stray dog palaces—earned him the nickname *"Inukubō,"* or "Dog Shōgun." His fondness for dogs is attributed to a superstitious nature—he was born in the Year of the Dog. It is a matter of historical record that the Naka-

no kennels sheltered over a hundred thousand dogs at one time.

bogey tale to frighten kids
Literally, "You're telling me a scary story, like the ballad about Sanshō the Bailiff." Sanshō the Bailiff is a legendary villain, about whom Mori Ōgai wrote a story and the director Mizoguchi made a film.

Page 128 **woman's "blood storm"**
In the original, *chi no michi*, or "path of blood." A somewhat archaic-sounding colloquialism with two meanings: 1. Blood vessel, vein. 2. Female hysteria arising from menstrual cycle. Cf. English "hysteria" from the Greek for "womb."

Ōkubo
Between Shinjuku and Nakano in modern Tōkyō.

Lord Maeda
The original describes him as *hyakuman koku no Maeda*, or "the Maeda whose income is a million *koku* a year." This is far beyond a mere million dollars, as a *koku* was the equivalent of a year's ration for a whole family (about forty-eight gallons). Maeda Tsunanori (1642–1724) is most probably the one referred to.

Yonekura
The Yonekura family came from Kai and was distantly connected with the Takeda family. Lord Yonekura was another of the shōgun's personal retainers.

Tōdō
A descendant of Tōdō Takatora, a famous general of the Momoyama era (1568–1600), first under Hideyoshi then under Ieyasu (see note for page 135), who gave him a fief in Ise and Iga worth 32,000 *koku*.

Page 129 **Nakano**
Presently the ward of Nakano in Tōkyō, west of Shinjuku.

Chief Abbot Ryūkō, at the Temple of Holy Prayer
Ryūkō (1649–1724) was appointed chief abbot of the Temple of Holy Prayer (Gojiin Genrokuji) in 1695. It was built by Shōgun Tsunayoshi in the Kanda district of Edo in 1688, and was his favorite temple. He visited it more than twenty times during his lifetime, but when it burned down in 1717, Shōgun Yoshimuné decided not to rebuild it and gave the name Gojiin to another temple. Since one possible meaning of Goji is "prayer," we have chosen this version to break the monotony of too many Japanese names, and to underline the irony of references to "mercy."

Page 130 **Sanctuary of Mercy**
In the Japanese, Jishinin. The Jishinin is part of the Kiyomizudera
temple complex in Kyōto. The author seems to have confused it with
the Jiganin, which is part of the Hasedera.

Hasedera temple
One of the oldest temples in Japan, founded c. 733 and later associated
with the Shingon (True Word) sect. It is situated in the Hasé district
of Sakurai City, modern Nara Prefecture, and is consecrated to Kan-
non, the Goddess of Mercy.

Shōdaiji
A short form for Tōshōdaiji, the mother temple of the Ritsu sect in
Nara. It was built by the Chinese monk Ganjin (of whom a famous
portrait statue exists) in 759. Shōgun Tsunayoshi and his mother en-
dowed it with a fund to repair the building in 1692.

Page 133 **Numazu**
An important town on the Tōkaidō road, made famous by Hiroshige's
prints. It was one of fifty-three post stations (*shukuba*) between Edo
and Kyōto which provided fresh horses, litter bearers, inns, and
teahouses (i.e. brothels) for travelers.

Page 134 **Nichiren**
One of the sages of Japanese Buddhism (1222–82) and founder of
the Nichiren sect. Claiming that his *satori* (enlightenment) came from
his understanding that the Lotus Sutra was the essence of true religion,
he severely criticized other sects. Since he also attacked the shogunate,
he was twice exiled—to Izu and later to Tosa in Shikoku. In his old
age, he spent several years in retreat at the monastery on Mt. Minobu
(see note for page 125). The Nichiren prayer (*daimoku*) consists of
the seven characters *na-mu-myō-hō-ren-ge-kyō* (as heard at the beginning of Kurosawa's film *Dōdes'ka-den*).

"Buddha have mercy on us"
In the original, *nembutsu*, a contraction of the invocation used by
the Jōdo (Pure Land) sect: *Namu Amida Butsu*, which might also be
rendered "Hail to the Buddha Amida."

Ryūōmura
Normally we do not translate local names, but in this case the reader
should know the underlying meaning, since water deities play an important part in the imagery of this story. Ryūō, or the Dragon King,
is the Far Eastern version of Neptune. His palace was believed to lie
at the bottom of the ocean, and in it lived his daughter, the beautiful
princess Otohimé (see note for Urashima Tarō, page 140). Dragons

generally are creatures of the air, of wind and rain, and through rain, of wave and water. Their properties are fundamentally benign, but they symbolize the power of the elements over the strongest animals, and to see one in its entirety is to court death (e.g. the waterspout—tatsumaki, or "dragoncoil"—in our story). Dragons are believed to be fond of eating sparrows and swallows.

Page 135 **cormorants**
In Japan, birds trained to dive for fish attracted to the surface by the light of torches, and carry them back to the boat in their gullets. They are kept on leashes, and rings around their necks prevent them from swallowing their prey. The cormorant fishermen of Nagarakawa in the province of Mino (modern Gifu) were famous for their proficiency in this old technique.

Takeda Shingen
The legendary warlord (1521–73) of the Muromachi period. A military genius at the age of twenty, he chased his own father to Suruga Province and consolidated his native domain of Kai. He then encroached on neighboring Shinano by defeating the local daimyōs. By the end of his life, he controlled almost all of central Japan, and could defy even the mighty Oda Nobunaga. In 1572 he defeated the army of Tokugawa Ieyasu (see note below), but before he could translate this military victory into a political one, he died in the field. Although he is remembered chiefly for his military exploits, he was a just administrator, introducing many of the principles of a stable, prosperous economy. Kurosawa's recent film, *Kagemusha* (The Shadow Warrior), depicts his life and times.

Tokugawa Ieyasu
The founder (1542–1616) of the Tokugawa shogunate. He was the last of the three statesmen who unified Japan after centuries of civil war. He appears in James Clavell's historical novel *Shōgun* as "Toranaga." See A. L. Sadler's *The Maker of Modern Japan*, London, 1937.

Page 137 **Jōruri**
A form of recitative (*katarimono*) to the accompaniment of the shamisen. Beginning in the Muromachi era, it developed through the Edo period and spread among the common population. At this time, it was used in puppet theater, Kabuki, and Japanese dance (*Nihon buyō*), as well as in solo performances. It had many schools, such as *Gidayū*, *Tokiwazu*, *Shinnai*, and *Kiyomoto*.

Page 139 **senior concubine**
The Japanese term might more accurately be rendered "lady-in-

166

waiting," but since it sounds odd for a *man* to have a lady-in-waiting, we give it as "concubine" in the sense of a secondary wife or "official" mistress. The relation, in other words, is not that of a casual liaison.

Page 140 **Urashima Tarō**

The hero of a popular legend, with aspects of both Rip van Winkle and Pandora. A young fisherman helps a sea turtle in distress, and the grateful animal takes him to the Dragon King (Ryūō—see note for page 134) in his palace at the bottom of the sea. Here he spends a pleasant year with its beautiful princess, Otohimé. Eventually getting homesick, he is given leave to go, after receiving from the princess a present of a beautifully carved box, which he is warned never to open. Carried back to his native shore—again by the turtle—he finds all the people who knew him are gone, since a hundred years of real time have passed. One day he opens the princess's box: a puff of smoke escapes from it and in an instant Tarō is an old man on the verge of death.

Asama Shrine

A Shintō shrine on Mt. Asama, one of the most active volcanoes in Japan. It served as a center for propitiation of the fire deities, and issued all kinds of protective amulets and the like.

Ibuse's Historical Fiction

1930–38	*Sazanami gunki*	"Waves: A War Diary"
1930	*Oranda dembō kimmizu*	"The Café from Holland"
1934	*Aokejima taigaiki*	"A General Account of Aokejima"
1937	*Sujō gimmi*	"The Family Tree Investigation"
1937	*John Manjirō hyōryūki*	"John Manjirō: A Castaway's Chronicle"
1938	*Biwazuka*	"The Biwa Mound"
1938	*Yujima fūzoku*	"The Mores of Yujima"
1939	*Yama o mite rōjin no kataru*	"An Old Man's Mountain Tale"
1939	*O-hori ni kansuru hanashi*	"The Story of the Moat"
1940	*Kawai sōdō*	"The Kawai Riot"
1940	*Enshin no gyōjō*	"Mementos of a Robber"
1943	*Fukigoé no shiro*	"The Castle of Fukigoé"
1946	*Futatsu no hanashi*	"Two Tales"
1946	*Wabisuké*	"Isle-on-the-Billows"
1949	*Toramatsu nisshi*	"The Toramatsu Journal"
1950	*Oshima no zonnengaki*	"A Geisha Remembers"
1952	*Yakushidōmae*	"In Front of the Inner Shrine of Yakushi"
1953	*Karusan yashiki*	*The Karusan Mansion*
1953–54	*Azuchi seminario*	"The Seminary of Azuchi"
1953	*Noheji no Mutsugorō ryakuden*	"The Life of Noheji Mutsugorō"
1954–55	*Hyōmin Usaburō*	*Usaburō the Drifter*
1955	*Kappa sōdō*	"The Water Imp Riot"
1955	*Kaikon mura no Yosaku*	"Yosaku the Settler"
1961	*Bushū hachigatajō*	"The Castle of Hachigata in Bushū"

Ibuse's Works Available
in English Translation

Hakuchō no uta. "Swan Song." Tr. by G. W. Sargent. *Eigo Seinen*, v. 102, nos. 9–12, 1956.

Henrō yado. "Pilgrims' Inn." Tr. by John Bester. *Lieutenant Lookeast, and Other Stories.* Tokyo, Kodansha International, 1971; London, Secker and Warburg, 1971. Pp. 53–58.

Honjitsu kyūshin. "No Consultation Today." Tr. by Edward Seidensticker. *Japan Quarterly*, v. 8, no. 1, 1961. Pp. 50–79. *No Consultation Today.* Tokyo, Hara Shobō, 1964. Pp. 8–123.

John Manjirō hyōryūki. "John Manjiro, the Cast-away." Tr. by Hisakazu Kaneko. Tokyo, Hokuseido, 1940.

Kaikon mura no Yosaku. "Yosaku, the Settler." Tr. by John Bester. *Lieutenant Lookeast, and Other Stories.* Tokyo, Kodansha International, 1971; London, Secker and Warburg, 1971. Pp. 113–29.

Kakitsubata. "The Crazy Iris." Tr. by Ivan Morris. *Encounter*, v. 6, no. 5, 1956. Pp. 92–93.

Kan'ya. "A Cold Night." Tr. by George Saito. *Japan P. E. N. News*, no. 18, March 1966. Pp. 1–6.

Kappa sōdō. "Catching a Kappa, or Water Imp." Tr. by Kiyoaki Nakao. *Two Stories by Masuji Ibuse.* Tokyo, Hokuseido, 1970. Pp. 4–28.

Koi. "Carp." Tr. by John Bester. *Lieutenant Lookeast, and Other Stories.* Tokyo, Kodansha International, 1971; London, Secker and Warburg, 1971. Pp. 91–95.

Kuroi ame. *Black Rain.* Tr. by John Bester. *Japan Quarterly*, v. 14, nos. 2–4, 1967; v. 15, nos. 1–3, 1968.

Black Rain. Tr. by John Bester. Tokyo, Kodansha International, 1969; London, Secker and Warburg, 1971.

Noheji no Mutsugorō ryakuden. "The Life of Mutsugoro of Noheji." Tr. by Kiyoaki Nakao. *Two Stories by Masuji Ibuse.* Tokyo, Hokuseidō, 1970. Pp. 32–72.

Noriai jidōsha. "The Charcoal Bus." Tr. by Ivan Morris. *Modern Japanese Stories,* ed. by I. Morris. London, Spottiswoode, 1961; Tokyo, Tuttle, 1962. Pp. 212–22.

Sanshōuo. "The Salamander." Tr. by Tadao Katayama. *The Reeds*, v. 2, 1956. Pp. 51–64.

"The Salamander." Tr. by Leon Zolbrod. *The East*, v. 1, no. 2, 1964. Pp. 21–23.

"Salamander." Tr. by Sadamichi Yokoo and Sanford Goldstein. *Japan Quarterly*, v. 13, no. 1, 1966. Pp. 71–75.

"Salamander." Tr. by John Bester. *Lieutenant Lookeast, and Other Stories.* Tokyo, Kodansha International, 1971; London, Secker and Warburg, 1971. Pp. 59–65.

Tajinko mura. "Tajinko Village." Tr. by John Bester. *Lieutenant Lookeast, and Other Stories.* Tokyo, Kodansha International, 1971; London, Secker and Warburg, 1971. Pp. 135–247.

Tangé shi tei. "At Mr. Tange's." Tr. by Sadamichi Yokoo and Sanford Goldstein. *Literature East and West*, v. 13, nos. 1–2, 1969. Pp. 167–81.

"Life at Mr. Tange's." Tr. by John Bester. *Lieutenant Lookeast, and Other Stories.* Tokyo, Kodansha International, 1971; London, Secker and Warburg, 1971. Pp. 97–111.

Ushitora jiisan. "Old Ushitora." Tr. by John Bester. *Lieutenant Lookeast, and Other Stories.* Tokyo, Kodansha International, 1971; London, Secker and Warburg, 1971. Pp. 67–89.

Yane no ue no sawan. "Sawan on the Roof." Tr. by Yokichi Miyamoto with Frederic Will. *Chicago Review*, v. 19, no. 1, 1966. Pp. 51–54.

"Sawan on the Rooftop." Tr. by Tadao Katayama. *The Reeds*, v. 11, 1967. Pp. 127–34.

"Savan on the Roof." Tr. by John Bester. *Lieutenant Lookeast, and Other Stories.* Tokyo, Kodansha International, 1971; London, Secker and Warburg, 1971. Pp. 129–34.

Yofuke to ume no hana. "Plum Blossom by Night." Tr. by John Bester. *Lieutenant Lookeast, and Other Stories.* Tokyo, Kodansha International, 1971; London, Secker and Warburg, 1971. Pp. 11–22.

Yōhai taichō. "A Far-worshipping Commander." Tr. by Glenn Shaw. *Japan Quarterly*, v. 1, no. 1, 1954. Pp. 53–73. *No Consultation Today.* Tokyo, Hara Shobō, 1964. Pp. 126–213.

"The Far-worshipping Commander." Tr. by Glenn Shaw. *The Shadow of Sunrise*, ed. by Shoichi Saeki. Tokyo, Kodansha International, 1966; London, Ward Lock, 1966. Pp. 157–86.

"Lieutenant Lookeast." Tr. by John Bester. *Lieutenant Lookeast, and Other*

Stories. Tokyo, Kodansha International, 1971; London, Secker and Warburg, 1971. Pp. 23–51.

Bibliography

Lifton, R., "Black Rain," *Death in Life* (1967), pp. 543–55.

Kimball, A., "After the Bomb," *Crisis in Identity and Contemporary Japanese Novels* (1973), pp. 43–59.

Liman, A. V., "Ibuse's Black Rain," in Tsuruta, K., and Swann, T., eds., *Approaches to the Modern Japanese Novel* (1976), pp. 45–72.

Liman, A. V., "Carp," "Pilgrim's Inn," in Swann, T., and Tsuruta, K., eds., *Approaches to the Modern Japanese Short Story* (1982), pp. 83–101.